When I Was Your Mother

a Novel

BY LIORA CARMELI

Producer & International Distributor
eBookPro Publishing
www.ebook-pro.com

When I Was Your Mother
LIORA CARMELI

Copyright © 2024 Liora Carmeli

All rights reserved; no parts of this book may be reproduced or transmitted in any form or by any means, electronic or mechanical, including photocopying, recording, taping, or by any information retrieval system, without the permission, in writing, of the author.

Translation: Monique Goldwasser
Editing: Nancy Alroy

Contact: yodfatc@bezeqint.net
ISBN 9798878749244

Chapter 1

Rain was pouring down when I reached the parking lot of "Ha-Kfitz" [The Spring], the plant where I worked. I turned around to look in the back seat of the car to see if I had possibly left an umbrella there, but I hadn't. I sighed, turned off the windshield wipers, let the heavy drops of rain run in rivulets down the windshield, and sank into the seat. I left the motor running for the heater to keep working.

I took out my cellphone and called my Aunt Ruth. No answer. Maybe she had already gone into a meeting and muted her phone.

The interior of the windshield fogged up and it was becoming difficult to see anything through it.

Maybe someone would notice that I had arrived and would come and save me with their open umbrella. No. Actually, it would be better if they didn't. Alone in the car and unable to get out, I felt that this might be a rare moment of grace, and I should use it to allow my thoughts to wash over me, letting them come and go as they pleased.

But the rain did not let up and, even with rain pouring down on the outside and steam misting up on the inside, I could still make out something through the windshield – a blurred form crossing the parking lot and hurrying to the front door.

I curled up and sank further down into the seat. Because I was such a stickler for punctuality, I still had five minutes until, officially, I had to stamp my time card.

Who would have thought that one day I would have to stamp a time card at a manufacturing plant for springs?

I smiled to myself as I remembered the arrogant look on my husband, Gil's, face when he saw me here in the plant for the first time. This was two weeks after I had been hired to work in the "Ha-Kfitz: Rosenblatt and Sons" family factory.

I was standing next to the window in the Quality Control room examining the spaces between the spring bindings of a medium-sized steel spring using a caliper, an exact calibrating instrument. When I finished and signed off on it, whereby giving my approval that work could continue, I raised my eyes and saw Gil standing across from me, wide-eyed and mouth agape. My soulmate looked so out of place on the production floor with all the manufacturing lines scattered about, operated by a workforce dressed in blue uniforms with oil on their hands while he was incongruously dressed in a suit and tie and a white, fresh shirt – one of many that he would meticulously iron every morning. I couldn't help it, I burst out laughing.

His face froze and then melted in a warm smile. "Maya... I still can't believe it," he said, being careful not to come too close to me so that he wouldn't stain his shirt.

"Life is full of surprises," I said and fumbled in my bag to find his wallet, which, for some odd reason, seemed to have found its way there.

"The best surprises are those we prepare for ourselves."

I gave him his wallet and he stood around aimlessly for a moment, as if trying to decide between two courses of action; he was staring at me like he was, once again, seeing me for the first time.

Rosenblatt, the father, passed by us, stopped, and turned around. I introduced him to Gil.

"Aha, the one from the halls of justice, if I am not mistaken." He said this in his usual derisive and dramatic tone.

"Something like that," Gil replied curtly.

"And he probably wants to make sure that every 'T' is crossed and every 'I' is dotted," my employer pointed out.

Gil was embarrassed. "I try. After all, I'm only just beginning as a lawyer," he said, trying to shake off the weight of the burden that Rosenblatt had placed on his shoulders.

"Today a lawyer, tomorrow a judge. Time moves fast, young man."

Gil smiled and said that, as far as time goes, he agreed with him completely and therefore, he should get going because he had a client waiting for him at the courthouse and the hearing would be starting in less than an hour.

Gil smiled at me and left. The wrinkles on his shirt from having sat in the car swooshed around on his back as he quickly left me, taking rapid steps. A tall man with broad shoulders, but not exaggeratedly so, not the result of bodybuilding in a gym. A man who was the love of my life.

Fate brought us together when we were 18 years old and I have cherished that precious moment ever since, enjoying the memory in good moments and drawing comfort from it in difficult times.

We were dancing at a Hanukkah party, each with a different group of dancers, and our eyes kept meeting. Something in his eyes, his expression, tugged at my heart. The distance between us narrowed, widened, and sometimes we accidentally bumped into each other. Every cell in my body was drawn to him, every inch of me was exposed to him. He danced as if possessed and, every once in a while, would throw his arms around in an involuntary movement, apparently expressing restrained enthusiasm, his eyes speaking to mine the whole time. Sweat beaded his brow and I longed to reach out with my arm and touch it but, instead, I brushed the drops of perspiration from my own forehead.

The music sped up and became more intense and the dance floor was even more crowded. We were flung against each other and now were dancing closer, the scents of our sweat intermingling, our lips turned up in a smile, trying to decipher the other's gaze.

"Your husband is adorable," Rosenblatt pointed out, sighing. "I always hoped that at least one of my sons would become an attorney, but they were both convinced that this plant is a gold mine and have been clutching onto it for dear life."

"You should be glad. Your sons are following in your footsteps, honoring what you built with your own hands."

"I'm certain that what really interests them is money, not creating something," Rosenblatt said with contempt, disappointment evident in his eyes.

"I'm certain that both can be true."

"Young lady, you've been here for two weeks and you already have an opinion! Do you have a magic spell for making money?"

I swallowed the rebuke but replied without hesitation, "If we improve the quality control process and meet the strict requirements – new market opportunities will open up and we'll be able to export to other countries…"

"That's enough! Get back to work. He who is careful will stay far away from all kinds of standards and permits," he grumbled.

"I thought that you would appreciate someone who insists on crossing every 'T' and dotting every 'I!'" I simply couldn't help myself.

"Young lady, I was talking about a fair trial and you are talking about steel springs," and with this, he turned his back to me and walked towards his office overlooking the production floor. I felt I had been scolded like a little girl who had tried to steal a toy.

Chapter 2

A few days later, Gil and I went out to dinner at an Italian restaurant to celebrate our wedding anniversary. We had reserved a table for two. I blinked, and the tall palm plant behind Gil looked as if its leaves were growing out of his head. I was reminded of the psalm that became a popular dance – *'Tzadik ka-tamar yifrach'* [A righteous man will bloom like the date palm] – and smiled to myself.

Gil smiled too, maybe in response to my smile or maybe from some inner association of his own.

I glanced around, my eyes roaming from him to the quiet, almost empty restaurant. In a distant corner of the room, the waiters were laying a tablecloth on a long table and arranging table settings. Across from me, Gil was eating with gusto, occasionally reaching over to taste something from my plate.

Because of the din of chairs being moved around and the murmuring, I raised my eyes once again and saw the three Rosenblatt men entering the restaurant accompanied by three women, who I imagined were their wives.

"My bosses just arrived," I said in a low voice. "Behind you. Don't turn around."

"Really? All three of them?" he asked.

"With their wives."

"Wow!" he responded.

"The father's wife is a psychologist," I said.

"Maybe that's why he uses pat phrases and quotes when he speaks, instead of using his own words."

"The wife of the older son, Eric, is also a psychologist; and the youngest, Daniel's wife, is an accountant."

"They're all educated," he pointed out.

After a brief silence, Gil began to tell me about a client who was calling him every day to check if there was any development in his case. "At the end of each conversation, he thanks me for my patience and says that he has never known such a polite young man."

"So, he only calls because he enjoys the fact that he has found a young man who is polite and patient."

"Or, he's testing my limits."

"And what are your limits?"

Gil looked at me, speared the last of the fettuccine swimming in the sauce on my plate with his fork, and slowly put it in his mouth.

I took a swig of the wine and, once again, glanced at my employers seated at the nearby table.

"Why don't you go and say hello?" asked Gil, aware of my curious glances.

"No, why should I? I wouldn't feel comfortable doing that."

"My wife? Shy?" he asked, smiling.

"Perhaps. What do you say about dessert?" I asked hurriedly. I tried not to look in their direction again. I concentrated on the dessert menu and, in the end, ordered the apple pie. Gil chose the chocolate cake.

"We're always so true to apples and chocolate," I commented.

"Loyalty is an essential virtue, is it not?"

We didn't speak on the way to the car or even after we got in it. Gil put on a playlist of quiet songs. The caressing voice of Mercedes Sosa penetrated every cell of my body and enveloped me like a warm and cozy blanket.

"Where are we going?" I asked when I noticed that he hadn't made the turn towards home.

"I don't know. It's still early."

I shut my eyes. I opened them when the car stopped but couldn't tell where we were.

"Come on, let's walk around a bit," said Gil.

I only saw the boats when I got out of the car.

"Is this the Herzliya marina?" I asked, hesitantly.

"I always knew I'd marry a woman who knows her surroundings."

Gil put his arm around my shoulder and, together, we walked along the pier. The port was so quiet with only the sound of the waves gently rocking the yachts.

"We'll own one of these one day," announced Gil with confidence. He had always dreamed of sailing far away, alone, in a small boat.

"Then we'll be perfect yuppies," I snickered.

"Don't exaggerate. I may be an attorney but you work in a factory."

"Does that bother you? Does it damage your image?" I asked, suddenly afraid to hear his answer.

"Doesn't it bother you? Aren't you sorry that you gave up the idea of studying at the university?"

"I certainly don't regret the children." Our sons, Dor and Shai were five and four, and Ya'ara, our daughter, was two years old.

"No disagreement there."

We continued to walk quietly between the sleeping yachts. "Look, there's a spring here!" Gil pointed beyond the prow of the boat closest to us. Attached to the three-strand rope that tied the boat to the dock was a large silver spring, intended to ease the movement of the vessel as it was being pulled and allowing it to sway freely.

"It's a sign," I said, sounding victorious.

Gil smiled at me.

The crescent of the moon hung over the masts of the quiet ships, surrounded by stars. The fleet in the sky looked down forgivingly upon the fleet owned by the rich of Herzliya and its surroundings.

I pushed my hand into the rear pocket of Gil's pants and he placed his hand on the nape of my neck, stroking my hair. The guard making his rounds didn't bother us with questions, apparently used to couples visiting the small port for a romantic stroll.

Chapter 3

I listened to the drum solo of the driving rain pouring down on the roof of the car, rhythmically accompanying my reverie back in time. Through the weeping windows, I could see blurred, indistinct figures – human legs on the bottom, an umbrella on top. My mind wandered and imagined that had we been created that way, we would always be protected from the rain and the scorching sun. Someone rapped on the window. I looked around and saw that it was Elena, who worked with me on quality control. She was hunched under an orange umbrella and gestured for me to join her. I smiled at her, shut off the engine, grabbed my purse, and jumped out of the car.

We huddled under the orange canopy and hurried to the plant's entrance. Elena walked in front of me, holding the dripping umbrella away from her short skirt, her high heels tapping out a rhythm. Her long legs aroused great interest from her fellow employees on a daily basis: the rate of visits to the quality control room had almost doubled since Elena began working there six months ago. I would come to work wearing jeans, a T-shirt or sweatshirt, shod in comfortable sneakers.

"I already checked last night's springs. No problems," said Elena.

"That's good." I went to my desk, turned on the computer, and brought up the file containing the regulations that I had been working on for the past few months.

Elena asked me if I'd be working on them today as well.

"Today, tomorrow, and the day after that too. Until I finish them."

"So I'll be alone at the window again?" she said, half asking, half grumbling.

I was well aware of her reservations: that I was not a full participant in the daily quality assessments, but rather devoted most of my time to writing the regulations and standards book. My goal was to bring the plant up a level where it would meet the strictest international standards, which would then put Rosenblatt and Sons on the frontline with the most advanced manufacturers in the world. When I began this project, I had no inkling that my biggest adversaries to achieving this goal would be the owners themselves.

In spite of the objections of the father and Daniel, the younger son, I continued my work as planned. I had no intention of putting aside everything that I had learned in the year-long course I had taken at the Institute of Labor Productivity just because one was pigheaded and the other, a mule!

In my mind's eye, I could already see modern measuring instruments being purchased, machines on the factory floor being relocated to their new homes, and the necessary steps being taken to make the plant more efficient.

After working on the computer for four hours, I leaned back in my chair, picked up the phone, and called Ruth. She still wasn't answering. I sent her a WhatsApp message, asking her to please call me.

I felt my belly rumbling and was debating whether to get a sandwich at the nearby sandwich shop or just add boiling water to the meals-in-a-cup I kept in my drawer – neither option sounded especially appetizing – when the door of the control room opened and in stepped Danny Katzir, the agent for the large kibbutz plant that manufactured components for irrigation and one of our biggest clients.

That's great, I thought. This is the perfect solution for lunch.

I suspected that he had timed his arrival in the hopes of enjoying a 'business lunch' and I went along with this, following specific instructions from Rosenblatt, the father, as to how to conduct ourselves with important clients: "Guests are to be treated even better than the divine presence. How does one receive guests? With food and drinks."

As far as I was concerned, Danny wasn't only a client. He also played an important role in my battle to introduce standards.

Only a month ago he had told me that the kibbutz was planning to begin exporting irrigation components and, as an aside, pointed out that the customer would insist that all parts meet strict international standards.

"How are you?" asked Danny, examining my face with his piercing eyes. "Haven't you your employers suggested yet that you wear something more professional than jeans?" he asked, smiling at Elena and, at the same time, gawking at her long, bare legs.

"Watch out they don't accuse you of sexual harassment," pointed out Eric, who had just entered the room.

"Once, it was a pleasure to compliment a woman, but now... one mustn't open one's mouth and one must keep one's eyes closed," responded Danny.

"Danny, you must be hungry," I said, trying in vain to change the subject.

"It depends on the hunger."

"A hunger that I can satisfy," I said, and immediately regretted my words.

He smiled at me salaciously.

I looked away from him, right into Eric's eyes, that were glaring at me. Suddenly I made a connection with other looks he had thrown my way from time to time and felt my cheeks flush.

I turned my attention back to the client and, in as businesslike a tone as I could muster, asked "A meal-in-a-cup from my drawer or David's Grill?"

"Neither, I have someone waiting for me in the car. I have to go."

Instead of a respite in a restaurant, I would have to make do with the ready-to-eat noodles and keep wondering about the meaning of Eric's gaze.

I had liked Eric – a man in his mid-thirties, average height, with wavy, black hair and dark eyes – since my first day at the job. He was patient and friendly, the only one who understood the importance of making improvements in quality control measures. During my job interview, I focused primarily on answering his questions because his father confused me with his fanciful language and Daniel's sour face put me off. Eric asked simple questions and listened to my answers with an encouraging expression.

Sometimes he would stay behind in the quality control room to talk to me. I never attached too much importance to that, nor to the looks that he would throw my way every once in a while but, for some reason, today, his glance discomfited me.

I poured boiling water over the Chinese noodles.

"Do you have one for me too?" he asked, sitting down on the chair across from me. Without a word, I opened another box of Chinese noodles, poured boiling water over them and closed the lid.

Chapter 4

On the ride home, I turned the radio channel to 'Gimel' [a popular radio station]. Miri Mesika was singing with bewitching wistfulness and her voice filled the small space, where only I was breathing the oxygen. Her voice put me in sync with an emotion that often tugged at my heart in the wee hours of the night, when I was lying there silently, awash with memories and worries, and something else which could not be defined with words.

Ruth still hadn't returned my call, I thought. I wondered what was holding her up. Apparently, she was having another busy day at work.

The last notes of the song faded away and Shlomo Bar's voice suddenly came on, singing "Children are joy, children are a blessing."

Why this song? I shut the radio off.

Whenever I walked down the street, my eyes would constantly be searching, moving to and fro, refusing to obey me when I ordered them not to look at the faces of children of a certain age.

I turned the radio on again, but even the deafening hail that had begun to beat down on the car roof could not drown out the insistent mantra of Shlomo Bar's song, "Children are joy, children are a blessing."

When I first started working at the plant, Eric brought his son with him to work one day. My eyes were irresistibly drawn to the bright-faced boy. His face was surrounded by curls and he had a shy smile.

I returned his smile and asked him how old he was.

"Nine," he replied in a soft voice.

I instinctively tensed up. Nine years old!

"Do you have any brothers or sisters?" I asked.

"No," he answered, a bit taken aback.

My heart skipped a beat. An only son! Nine years old!

I examined his features over and over, each feature separately and all of them as a whole. For a moment, I could see a resemblance – the chestnut-colored hair like Gil's, the shape of his nose similar to mine? – and then dismissed it all. But when he smiled at his father, his smile looked so familiar. I was flooded with emotions.

I guess I didn't do a very good job of hiding them. Eric saw the expression on my face and sent his son to look for 'interesting springs.' After the little figure had gone down the corridor and turned the corner, Eric explained, without my having asked, that after giving birth, his wife had developed an infection in the fallopian tubes and since then was unable to conceive, despite the many treatments she had undergone.

I felt relief wash over me, followed immediately by a sense of emptiness. I managed to mutter a few words of sympathy and some complimentary words about his son. Eric's face glowed with pride and he began to tell me about the boy's proficiency in taking things apart and reassembling them, about his ability to concentrate and about the interest he was showing in the machines and the springs they were manufacturing. "During vacations he comes to the plant quite often; he especially enjoys being in the warehouse, next to the automated equipment."

"He's welcome to come visit us in Quality Control," I said, managing a polite smile and returning to my office.

I regretted having asked the boy if he had siblings. I should have known better, as I remember the embarrassment I had felt as a young girl, and then as a teenager, every time someone asked me if I had a brother or a sister. I had been so happy when Gil sat in the once-empty chair at the table in my parents' house.

Pleasant thoughts about Gil were what reminded me of the meal-in-a-cup noodles that I had shared with Eric. "Let's play hooky from work one day and go eat a real meal in an Asian restaurant," he had suddenly suggested in a mischievous tone that was completely out of character with his usual solemn demeanor.

"Maybe… one day."

"You sound as if it's not an option," he teased me.

"Basically, everything is possible," I mumbled.

"Exactly. It all depends on what one wants," he said, sending that piercing look my way once again.

I was saved from the awkward conversation by Daniel, who had just entered the room.

"Wouldn't a good sandwich have been preferable?" he asked, making a face when he saw the empty plastic containers. He never overlooked an opportunity to criticize, to find something negative and to capitalize on it.

I tried to convince myself that I just imagining it, that there was no reason to place any importance on his occasional glances which might be perceived by some as flirting. But the truth was, both his actions and looks took me back to the past, to the time I had fallen in love with Gil.

The loud ringing woke me up out of a deep sleep the morning after the party. I opened the door, completely befuddled, and saw Gil standing in front of me. I had to catch my breath. I had fallen asleep on the living room couch and was still wearing the short black dress from the night before. Embarrassed, I ran my hand through my hair. It must be a real mess, I thought.

Gil looked refreshed. I studied him. He had a high forehead, short hair, and warm, dark eyes. The magic was still there. Whatever threads that had connected his heart and mine during the dancing had not been broken during the few hours of sleep.

"I didn't know that your brown eyes have flecks of green," he said.

The neighbors from across the hall opened their door and looked at us.

"Come in," I said to Gil and, with those words, I brought him into my life. He sat down on the couch while I went to take a shower and make myself more presentable. I looked in the mirror and pinched my cheeks to give them some color.

When I returned to the living room, I found him lounging comfortably on the easy chair, immersed in a book. I observed his face before he felt my presence – long, dark lashes and the small indentation left by his sunglasses on a straight and somewhat broad nose.

He raised his eyes and looked at me, and my heart did somersaults.

Chapter 5

Eric's image faded away. Once again, I turned on the radio and absent-mindedly listened to the news – traffic jams, traffic accidents; an old woman living alone had been robbed; negotiations between the government and the teachers' union had reached an impasse; even the weather forecast was not encouraging: strong winds, hail and cold. Couldn't they find one positive thing to report on among all this depressing news I grumbled to myself.

I switched to my playlist and gave myself up to the music. It succeeded in banishing my despondency but not the constant undertone of sadness that had been with me for so many years.

One day, a few months into our love story, Gil was fondling my breasts and said, "It looks as if they have grown because of me. It must be because I've cared for them like a gardener cares for his plants."

Two weeks later, it turned out that he had indeed been cultivating his garden, perhaps a little too well. My period was late. Apparently, the pill I was on, originally to prevent acne and, later, to prevent pregnancy, no longer worked for me and I'd have to change my prescription.

But when Dr. Chazan looked at the ultra-sound monitor, he told me straight out that he saw a fetus in my uterus. I protested and maintained that it couldn't be, I was protected. I had a safety net – the pill.

"Young lady," he said, "if you forget the pill even once, that safety net tears and the fish swim right through."

I was speechless. I wanted to escape from my body or, through some sort of magic, turn back time and invalidate the verdict. Then I turned my anger on myself – how could I have become pregnant in a modern era, with all the information and means? – which was immediately followed by a sense of guilt – how could I have been so irresponsible and forgotten to take the pill?

While I was getting dressed, I could hear Dr. Chazan from behind the curtain saying, "Come with your mother and we'll set a date for an abortion." The shoe I was holding dropped to the floor. "I'll prepare the documents for the committee," he finished.

I finished dressing and, instead of going to sit across from him, opened the door and left. He called out to me, telling me to come back, but I ignored him.

As we had agreed, Gil was waiting for me at the entrance to the building. He smiled at me. I gave him my hand and began walking quickly, pulling him after me.

Gil asked if we were trying to escape something or someone, and I answered that I wished it were possible. When I was forced to stop at a crosswalk because of a red light, Gil demanded an explanation for the rush.

I told him the news as curtly as the gynecologist had told me.

The light turned green and everyone had to go around us to cross the street. We both stood exactly where we were and looked at one another – Gil, in disbelief and shock and I, contrite and sad.

I let go of his hand as soon as the light turned green and stepped out into the street. I moved swiftly over the crosswalk's black and white lines and hurried along the sidewalk, weaving between passersby, and made a random right turn. I began running until I reached a construction site surrounded by a high fence. Gil arrived a minute later, embraced me and, together, we collapsed on a pile of sand.

"Have an abortion and we can forget this ever happened," he said to me, as if it was a foregone conclusion, taking it for granted.

"I am not going to have an abortion."

Gil was quiet. I knew what he was thinking. We were high school seniors with our army service still ahead of us. He had successfully passed the selection process for the paratroopers; I had been accepted to a course for instructors in the armored corps.

He had logic on his side, but I knew that under no circumstances would I agree to surgically scrape this miraculous connection between the ova and the sperm that had been created in my uterus.

"I will have the baby, and we will give it up for adoption," I said. I thought about Ruth, my favorite aunt. She would be willing to help me.

"Why?" he asked, raising his voice.

I kept silent.

"I don't understand! This is just the beginning of the pregnancy! It can be stopped and we can go on with our lives!"

I remained quiet. I found that I couldn't put into words what I was feeling deep down.

"Why?" he asked again, demanding an answer.

"Why? Because there are many couples who want children and cannot have any!" The words burst out from me as if I had come to this conclusion after giving it a lot of thought.

"So you want to save the world?"

"No, just one couple."

Gil took me in his arms and whispered in my ear, listing obvious arguments: think about your parents, what will they say? How will you finish the school year? What about the matriculation exams? What about your army service? And what about the pre-army trip to Greece that we had planned to take before going into the army?

I hugged him back and stayed silent.

In the end, he said that I would probably wake up the next day thinking differently, and that I would reach a logical, rather than an emotional, decision.

I felt a stab of unfairness and disappointment. What did I expect? That he would feel as I did?

My parents, both scientists, were about to go to the United States on a sabbatical and I was supposed to move in with Aunt Ruth. She was my mother's sister, 40 years old and single. I couldn't think of a better or more appropriate turn of events. She worked for the Ministry of Social Affairs in the Department of Child Welfare Services, the office that handled adoptions. I told her about the pregnancy and made her swear not to say one word about it to my parents. As expected, after recovering from the shock of the news, she tried in every way to convince me to do what one should do at my age – that is, to terminate the pregnancy – but I challenged all of her arguments.

Gil remained adamant about an abortion and put constant pressure on me, going from pleading to anger. In the end I gave in but kept putting off going to the doctor. Gil was furious. How dare I go against what we had decided? What I had promised? Frustrated, he berated me, saying that he had an equal role in this unplanned pregnancy, and the fact that it was happening in my body did not give me the right to make a unilateral decision.

I kept silent in the face of his accusations. I understood him; I knew that he was right and that I was being unfair, but I couldn't go along with his wishes or with the voice of reason.

Our love, our conversations, the good times we had had – everything that had seemed special and forever – faded away and disappeared. Before going to Italy with his parents and brothers as a reward for having completed the 12th grade, he once again tried to convince me to terminate the pregnancy. He pleaded. He cried. I cried too, feeling desperate because he didn't understand me, but it was this trying time together that renewed the love we had for each other that I thought had died and, in a moment of weakness – when we were pressed against each other in a desperate embrace – I promised to do as he asked. The reconciliation was sweet. Once in his arms again, I understood how much I would miss my beloved Gil, and us as a couple.

My parents flew to Boston, Gil flew to Rome, and I called the doctor. He made a last-minute appointment for me with the 'abortion committee,' because the window for a D&C was closing. I felt like a robot. The committee gave its approval and Ruth took me to the hospital. A nurse took me to a room and left so that I could remove my clothes and put on a hospital gown. When I sat down on the bed, I felt a flutter inside of me, like a sign, shouting "I am here." The apathy that had replaced my convictions since Gil had left, dissipated. I left the room and fled as fast as I could, like a heroine in a melodrama.

As soon as Gil returned from Italy he came to me and put his arms around me, ready to provide comfort and support after the difficult ordeal. When I informed him that I hadn't gone through with it, he froze, pulled away, turned on his heel and left. I didn't see him again. No calls, no text messages – he simply disappeared.

I texted him and left voice messages – maybe he would soften if he heard my voice – but in vain.

At that point, we were only going to school to take our matriculation exams. Occasionally I would see him with his friends. We ignored each other. My friends understood that we had broken up, but I refused to talk to them about it. I distanced myself from everyone and everything.

It felt good living at Ruth's. This wasn't the first time that my parents had gone away for a sabbatical year. When I was little, I would join them. Every few years we'd spend the year in a different country. For me, it meant a new school and long hours of being alone and very lonely. If I only had a brother or a sister… but, for my mother, when it came down to either a brilliant career or having another child, the career won out.

I was just about to begin the 7th grade when my parents excitedly told me that they were going abroad for another year, this time to carry out research at a prestigious university in England. Not only was I not infected with their scientific enthusiasm, but

I rebelled. I was not willing to forego the move to middle school or all the new friends that I expected to make. After many tears and bitter arguments, a solution was found – Ruth would take me in – and that's what happened. She took me under her wing and looked after me for a year.

Just like now.

Just as summer vacation began, my belly began to show.

Chapter 6

The next day I was, once again, in a line of cars trying to zig-zag my way through the snarled traffic. I refrained from calling Ruth. The previous evening, she had texted me saying that she had had a crazy day at work and that she would call me today. The radio was set to a local station and I let the silly dialogues interspersed with happy songs serve as a bridge between the morning with the family and a new day at work.

My phone rang as I entered the quality control room. It was Danny Katzir. His 'good morning' was terse and sharp and I immediately felt very anxious.

"I rejected the shipment that arrived yesterday," he informed me, without a preamble.

"What? The whole thing?" I was shaken up. This affected thousands of pieces.

"Yes, the springs are too short."

"How can that be?" I protested, and, in my mind, began to go over all the tests we had run on the springs which had been manufactured in accordance with the specifications of his order, intended for high-powered sprinklers. "We carried out all the necessary inspections," I said, trying to protect the springs, the plant's good name, and my professional reputation.

"I don't know what you did, but the springs I received do not comply with our order. At least, not all of them," he added.

"Wait a minute. What do you mean – not all of them?" I said, hope springing up.

"Some are too short and I do not intend to waste my people's time sorting them all out," he cut me off.

"Okay, I'll take care of it," I replied confidently but inside, I was thinking of all the wasted hours that would go into sorting them out and throwing an unknown number of springs into the recycling bin.

Elena saw my face cloud over and asked who had upset me on the phone. When I told her what had happened, she went out to the work floor and returned with the veteran operator who had manufactured the springs in question. "It can't be mine," he protested, "I brought them all in to be inspected and they were all approved!"

"And what about the ones that were manufactured during the night?"

His face lit up when he realized that maybe he'd be off the hook. "When I left and the night shift took over, the machine was operating properly. The rest is not my responsibility."

He was right, I thought, and told him that when the operator who had worked the night shift arrived he should be sent directly to me.

I would have to stay late and, if Gil wasn't available, I'd have to find some sort of arrangement for the children. There was no other choice; I had to check this out thoroughly, even at the cost of coming home late.

I reported the situation to Daniel. He frowned.

"I need someone to sort the springs."

"Are they here?" he asked, impatiently.

"Not yet. They'll be here at noon."

"So we'll talk at noon," he growled, and turned to go.

"If we had worked according to standards, this would not have happened," I couldn't help myself.

He turned his back to me and left.

At exactly 7:00 p.m., the veteran operator appeared at the quality control window accompanied by a young man; the bespectacled lad looked so young and thin. I had often passed him in the mornings, rushing to go home as I was hurrying to go in and start my day. Now he looked frightened, his eyes lowered behind his glasses. I waited for him to say something, but he was silent. It looked as if he wouldn't talk at all. Instead, the veteran worker spoke up.

"Rami said that the day before yesterday he had to leave early, so he placed the crates to the side and left."

"You skipped the inspection stage because you were hurrying to go home?" I demanded to know.

The young man nodded, embarrassed, and continued to look down.

"Answer me! Did you think that it was okay to leave early and skip the inspection stage?"

He raised his frightened eyes to me. "The springs are almost always satisfactory," he mumbled in a shaky voice.

"Almost. This time they were too short," I said, harshly. Don't pity him, I told myself.

He squirmed and looked as if he was about to collapse.

Proper procedures would have prevented this, I thought, and decided that I was not responsible for all of the plant's problems, placing that responsibility firmly on the broad and reluctant shoulders of Rosenblatt and Daniel. In any case, the boy would have to be fired. There was no room for compromise.

"It won't happen again, I swear," he pleaded, as if he was reading my mind.

I looked from him to the crates of rejected springs that were piled next to the quality control room. As expected, Daniel had not been in any hurry to send anyone to sort through them.

"Come at noon tomorrow and sort through all of these crates. You won't get paid for that." I had found a way out for him and also for the plant – partial compensation for the damage done. I could see in his eyes that he was hesitating. "If you don't come on time, consider yourself fired," I said.

Any reservations he had disappeared and his face showed gratitude. "I'll be here on time. Of course."

I left the plant at 8 p.m. I had been buried in my work all day, but now I had the time to call Ruth. She answered but said that she couldn't talk right then and promised to call me the next day. Once again, I wondered if she was avoiding me.

About half of the thousands of springs had to be thrown into the large recycling bin, but the other half could be repackaged and Danny Katzir was going to come and pick them up.

"You won't turn me down for lunch at 'Shipudei David' today, right?" I asked, in a light tone.

A smile spread over his face. "Turn you down? Why would I? Who can refuse you – or kebabs?"

"You did, a few days ago," I reminded him.

We sat across from each other in the crowded restaurant. At lunchtime, workers from all around the industrial area rushed towards the seductive aromas of the selection of meats that David grilled and the homemade dishes that his wife, Zehava, prepared in the kitchen in the back – stuffed vegetables, couscous and an array of salads.

Danny and I waited in line for our turn to receive the skewers that David was turning on the grill. Near us, two young men sitting at a table got up and left. My field of vision expanded and I saw Gil sitting a few tables away from me. He had his back turned to me, but I easily recognized his short hair touching the collar of his white shirt. A young woman was sitting across from him and, every once in a while, she would sensually toss her smooth hair back off her face with a movement of her head and expose her delicate features. A boy who seemed to be about ten years old was sitting with them, his shiny hair almost covering his eyes. Gil turned to him and I could see his profile. He smiled at the boy and stroked his shoulder.

The blood drained from my face and I stopped breathing. I was filled with burning jealousy. Who was that woman? Who was that boy? Could Gil have found the boy and hidden it from me? I knew it was a crazy thought, but…

She tossed her hair back once again and I was reminded of the long hair I had back then. When Gil and I met, he really liked my wavy, chestnut hair and asked me not to cut it short because he liked long hair. From that day on, no scissors had touched my hair and, at its longest, it had reached the small of my back. Even after we broke up, I didn't go to the hairdresser, not even while serving in the army or after I left the army. But one year after Dor was born and shortly before Shai's birth, I realized that taking care of my long hair took too much time and effort and I surprised myself by doing the unthinkable. When Gil arrived home, a new woman came to the door to greet him, with a carré cut just below my cheeks, framing my face in a different way. I was afraid of his reaction but he surprised me with compliments and genuine enthusiasm. In time, the hairdresser cut my hair shorter and shorter and Gil never reminded me that he found long hair more attractive.

So, who was this pretty woman with the long hair?

The waiter came over with a variety of salads and placed them on their table. They ate, talking all the while. She smiled. The boy pecked at his food.

"Hey, where did you go?" Danny's voice reached me, as if from another world.

I looked back at him and forced myself to smile and listen to him, but my eyes kept returning to Gil's back. I pretended that it was a target and was shooting one deadly arrow after another at it.

When our orders came, Danny began eating enthusiastically and, as always, it was accompanied by a string of jokes. With unusual skill, he was able to take a bite, chew, talk, and swallow, almost at the same time, and even burst into laughter.

"What is harder than a diamond?"

I didn't know. What did I know about diamonds?

"Paying for it!!" he said, his mouth full.

I had no appetite and thought that maybe, one day, I should bring Dor and Shai here so that they would know that French fries come in shapes other than those thin, fried things that they get with their fast-food kid's meals.

"Why did the boy draw on the window?" he continued, willingly accepting the skewer that I handed over to him from my plate.

"Because he wanted his picture to be clear!" Danny announced, gleefully.

"Boy? What boy?"

"The boy in the picture, of course!"

"Ah… of course."

Danny cleared his plate, leaned back, and was quiet. Eating and talking had tired him out, so he ordered coffee.

I looked at the boy sitting next to Gil and my mind was taken back to the days when I was pregnant.

For me, those days were a kind of respite; I was living in a bubble. I would lay in bed for hours, staring out the window of my room at Ruth's house at the old pine trees whose needles were reaching up to the blue sky, bracing against the force of the wind that was trying to knock them off.

I avoided my friends. Some had already started their army service and I avoided the others, coming up with excuses until they gave up inviting me out. Luckily, the date of my recruitment was later than theirs.

Every once in a while, I found myself writing WhatsApp messages to Gil and then erasing them before I sent them. I remembered the date he was supposed to go into the army and, on that day, I wrote him a long letter of apology, asking him to understand. But, in the end, I erased that one too.

Ruth was with me for the birth. The images of the baby being held up in front of me, his mouth open in a howl, and the midwife whisking him away did not leave me for days and nights after that. Until I enlisted. Then I was driven towards a much different life, that of a soldier. The new experiences occupied all of my attention.

My parents returned from their sabbatical in the middle of my army service and I returned home. The baby that I had given up for adoption remained in my past, in my previous life.

Chapter 7

I drank the coffee that Danny had ordered and was grateful for the temporary lull. My husband continued to carry out a lively conversation with the woman sitting opposite him, who was now gathering up her hair in a pin, exposing her pretty face even more. The boy also took part in the conversation and would often nod his head and smile. I felt as if I was going crazy. I wondered if this jealousy would dwell within me forever, if every time I saw him interacting with another woman, I would always be hit by the illogical, tangible, and concrete fear that he would leave me.

Danny didn't seem to notice the glances I was sending over his shoulder, but the pretty woman picked up on them and mentioned it to Gil.

He turned around and saw me. The happy smile that he sent my way pierced the balloon of suspicion that I had been blowing up. He came to our table and I introduced him to Danny. After a few polite words, Gil apologized and said that he had to go back to his client. He had an amused look in his eyes. I was sure that he was aware of what I had been imagining.

Why aren't you ever jealous when it comes to me? I once asked him. And I added that low-grade jealousy shows that the love is great, but he waved away the silly idea with a laugh and a kiss.

Gil went back to sit with the woman and the boy and I breathed a sigh of relief. I took a bite of the almond cookie that was served with the coffee and was thankful for everything I had – a wonderful husband, great children, an interesting job, good health. 'You have to be satisfied with what you have!' I told myself sternly. Your world is complete!

On the day I was discharged from the army, I was immersed in thoughts about the next phase of my life and all that I was leaving behind. I got off the bus and took the long way home, walking along small side streets. It was late afternoon when reached the public park next to my parents' home, enjoying the light autumn breeze. Someone was running towards me. I moved aside to let him pass. I heard the gurgling laughter of a baby and turned my head. A young man was lifting a baby up in the air. He had his back to me and the baby's face was facing me.

It stopped me cold in my tracks. In my mind, I was seeing another baby being lifted, his mouth open for his first breath. A naked baby, just born, with a wrinkled face, black tufts of hair covering a round head and eyes scrunched up in a grimace before he let out his first howl.

These images in my head were so clear, depicted in minute detail. My knees became weak. I sat down on a nearby bench covered with dry leaves and, for a long time, maybe an hour, did not move. The sun was sinking in the west, the shades of twilight had completely disappeared and the street lamps had been turned on. Feeling heavy, I rose and began walking towards the house.

Something changed in me that day. The khaki band-aid which had protected me for two years had been ripped off.

Return to civilian life was different from anything I had imagined or planned. I was struck by a sadness which I didn't know how to process. I lost my appetite. I couldn't sleep. The picture of the baby being held up in front of me – the squinty eyes, mouth wide open – refused to leave me. I tried to distract myself by meeting up with friends, by looking for temporary work, but found no solace.

Early one morning, after a week of deep sadness and sleepless nights, I called Ruth.

"Maya?" her voice was thick with sleep.

"Ruth, I want to know how my baby is."

"What baby?" I could tell from her voice that she hadn't woken up completely.

"The baby I had. My baby."

After a moment of silence, she said, her voice still muted but firm, "He isn't yours and I can't talk to you about him."

"I just want to know how he is. You're the only one who knows."

"I don't know anything." By this time, she was getting annoyed.

"I don't want to know any details about him, just how he's doing."

"Maya…"

"Only to know how he's doing, if he's healthy," I insisted.

"I can't talk to you about this!" her voice escalating into a shout.

"Are you hiding something from me? Is he sick? Is he dead?"

"God forbid. He's healthy."

"That's all I wanted to know. Thank you."

I hung up. At least that, I thought to myself. He's not mine, and will never be mine, but he is healthy.

I wanted to talk to someone about what I was going through, but Ruth was the only one who knew my secret. Too bad that my parents don't know, I thought. Maybe it was time to share this with them.

I went into their room but they were still sleeping. My father was lying on his side, snoring. My mother was on her back, covered up to her chin, earbuds in her ears.

My father had begun snoring the year before and, since then, she hadn't had a quiet night's sleep. She made a point of getting into bed before him and falling asleep before the overture started, but then she would wake up in the middle of the night and, after many failed attempts to fall back asleep, she'd have to move to the spare bed in the study so she could continue sleeping. My father refused to believe that it was as bad as she claimed until, one night, she recorded him and made him listen to the loud noises, the abrupt breaths and long, sawing snores that made up the shrill modern opus.

They subsequently tried a number of solutions, but nothing worked. In the end, she bought good quality earbuds and, since then, the playlists offered by Spotify enabled her to sleep, and all was well.

I looked at them for another minute, and my determination to disclose everything to them evaporated.

I sank into despair. I barely ate or slept. My heart was very heavy.

My parents thought that my depression was due to my discharge from the army, the pressure of having to begin living a 'real' life as an adult, choose a path, and decide what to study at the university. As scientists who were dependent upon data, numbers, and formulae, they both had clear directions in life and could focus on their aspirations. They expected me to follow in their footsteps and choose one academic field or another, but also wanted me to make an informed decision, not to choose rashly.

One day I awoke early. The weak, pre-dawn greyish light shone through the east window of the kitchen. I filled a glass with water and sat in front of the window, looking at the sun making its way from the southern to the northern hemisphere.

My father also had woken up early and made coffee for the both of us. He stood next to me, opposite the dazzling ball of light. "You're still finding it difficult," he said. Once again, I was tempted to tell him about the grandson that he would never know but, before I could do so, he continued, "I promise you that it will pass. Heartache is no different than a sore throat or an earache."

Instead of coming clean, I asked him if this was a scientific promise, supported by formulae and laboratory results, and he laughed and sipped his coffee.

What I wouldn't give to trade my despair for a terrible earache.

My practical mother decided that sports would help me. "You loved playing basketball when you were in high school, and you were great at it. In the 11th grade, you were even on the girls' varsity team," she reminded me. Then she added that she had made some inquiries and found out that Maccabi Tel Aviv had an amateur basketball team that met twice a week and would be happy to have a talented player like me join them.

She pointed out that physical activity raises the body's level of endorphins, which are the hormones responsible for feelings of happiness and well-being.

It was during one of those periods of well-being that Gil and I met again.

He had come to the club to pick up a fellow student. I had just finished practice and was on my way to the parking lot. My team shirt was damp with sweat, my face red from exertion and my hair was unkempt and damp. I preferred not to shower in the dressing room, but rather to go straight home and shower there. I was rummaging in my purse for my keys as I walked, and when I raised my head, I saw him striding in my direction. At the sight of him, the familiar feeling that used to wash over me overcame me once more, as if three years had not passed since we last saw each other.

My heart, which had slowed down after running back and forth between the baskets, began to beat intensely once again and my mouth went dry.

For just a moment, we were silent. Gil was the first to regain his composure, said "Wow," and how nice it was to see me; he guessed that I had probably been playing basketball and explained that he had come to pick up a friend who was studying law with him at the university. Then he asked what was going on with me and fell silent.

When I dared to look in his eyes, I could see that he was embarrassed. I had imagined a chance meeting between us a million times, but in none of the scenarios was I red and sweating from exertion. I replied that I was okay, that I was hurrying home and turned towards my Toyota. I felt his eyes on my wet, sweaty back.

After all this time, what a way for this to happen I thought, frustrated.

But it turned out that, for some reason, he liked seeing me all worn out and blushing. He called a few hours later. For the first time in many years his name appeared on my caller ID. There were many instances in which I had been on the verge of deleting his name and number from my contact list but, for some reason, hadn't gone through with it. I knew that he was no longer in my life, but I just couldn't delete him from my cellphone. Not even after friends who had been with us in high school made sure to let me know he had a serious girlfriend, someone he had met in the officers' training course. Not even when I, too, had had a boyfriend that I had met in the army, and especially not when I had broken up with him a few months later.

And now, his name and photo appeared on my phone's screen. I answered. He asked if I would meet with him and suggested a café by the sea, the one to which we had liked to go during our months of being in love. I agreed and, two hours later there we were, sitting across from one another at a small table. We caught up a bit and spoke about general things, but did not mention the pregnancy or the birth, the cause of our breakup. He was surprised to hear that I had not enrolled in law school, as had once been the plan, and I told him, briefly, about my 'post-army breakdown' that had held me back, the crisis I experienced when I was discharged from military service. Our mouths poured out facts and our eyes shone with emotions. The attraction between us was very powerful, just as it had been at that party where we first met.

Once again, we didn't go our separate ways. The depression I had been feeling dissipated and made room for joy and love. Our connection became stronger and I took hold of the 'elephant in the room' by its trunk and threw it out. I got rid of it and didn't mention it.

One evening when we were in my room, Gil asked when I planned to enroll in law school.

"I want to get married," I replied.

He was dumbfounded. He looked at me, expecting me to say that I was only joking.

"And have a baby," I added.

I had finally expressed aloud the thoughts and desires that had been a part of me ever since we had reunited.

Gil tried to thrust my words aside using logic – we were too young to be parents – after all, I was planning to study law, just like him, and we were going to travel abroad after we received our degrees. He couldn't understand how I could want to trade all of that for diapers and pacifiers.

Over the next few weeks, he tried to convince me that this was a passing fancy, that I should begin my law studies and, if after one year I still felt the same, we would reconsider the matter. However, I knew for sure that this was the only thing that would keep me happy. I felt a deep and suppressed depression coming on and was afraid it would raise its head. I felt that only a baby, or two, or three, would free me from the sorrow of that first baby.

In the end, he said that I was being stubborn – just like I had been then…

That was the first time that he had referred to 'then,' and I wanted to grab onto the Pandora's box he had opened – and spill out all that I was feeling, what was motivating me, and to share my innermost and most irrational thoughts with him.

But he plowed on without a pause and said, "Of course we'll marry one day and have children. But why now?"

I was just about to answer when he said, "I think that you should go to therapy."

"Because I want to get married and have children?"

Chapter 8

Gil, his client, and the child rose from the table. Gil turned in my direction, smiled, and waved. I smiled and waved back and suddenly asked myself whether he had ever cheated on me since we'd been married. The very thought frightened me. I felt my heart rising up in my throat. I picked up my cup of coffee, which had managed to cool down by then, and drank it all up. Then I poured in some of the water from the jug and drank that too, along with the coffee residue at the bottom of the glass.

Danny finished his coffee and, as if he had received an agreed-upon signal, began talking seriously about the sophisticated, small side springs that he wanted to examine when we returned to the plant.

I cleared my mind of all the nonsense that I had been thinking and tried to concentrate. "Look, I am trying to introduce standardized work procedures but it's not easy. I hope that, in the future, there will not be any more mishaps like the one this week."

"That's good," he replied, patting his full belly.

"I need your help for this."

"I spoke to Rosenblatt again, but the old man is stubborn," said Danny.

"Words won't help. Send a letter that says that, in order for you to be able to continue to work with us, we have to adhere to accepted standards." The image of Gil making love to a faceless woman was spinning in my mind's eye. I felt my face burning and drank more of the disgusting water.

"Are you alright?" he asked.

The mobile phone in my purse rang and saved me from answering. My mother was on the line. She spent three afternoons a week at our house. First she picked up Dor and Shai from their kindergarten, gave them lunch and put Shai down for a nap. Dor adamantly refused to shut his eyes during the day, so she'd read to him, usually a 'long book that would not finish fast.' Then, while he watched a children's TV show, she'd call to tell me how they are. When Ya'ara bus arrived home from daycare at 4 p.m., my mom was there to greet her.

Around the time Shai was born, my mother took early retirement from her job in the Physics Department at Tel Aviv University. "I want to be an active grandmother, one who is around," she explained. My father and I doubted that caring for young children could ever replace the fascinating world of academics to which she had dedicated her life for the past decades, but she was content with her decision and, ever since then, had certainly proven herself right.

Even the way she looked changed. When she was working, she had always been obsessed with how she looked: her hair-do, her make-up, her wardrobe. Now, she radiated a sense of calm simplicity. She had stopped straightening her curls, which now gave her a somewhat impish look, almost never put on make-up, and had replaced the tailored suits with loose pants and T-shirts. All of this earned the family's wholehearted approval and everyone agreed she was prettier this way.

Her willingness to help never ceased to surprise me; but what really filled me with warmth and gratitude was the connection that had developed between the two of us as a result of the love and attention she lavished on the children.

"She is compensating for all the times she wasn't around as a mother," I said to Gil at the beginning of this unexpected turn of events. I added in a doubtful tone, "let's see how long it lasts."

"She might surprise you," he said optimistically, and he was right.

Yesterday, she had gleefully quoted a brilliant comment that Dor had made. "The child is so smart," she said, full of pride.

"Oh, no! So there's a danger that one day he'll be a professor of nuclear physics?"

"He certainly won't work in a plant," she couldn't help herself, but softened her words when she saw my expression and added, "Shai is so athletic; maybe he'll be a basketball player."

Remembering yesterday's pleasant chitchat and, now, her brief report about the boys having been picked up from the kindergarten cleared my mind of all the nonsense that I had been imagining and had been in a hurry to believe. My heart filled with love for my parents, the children, Gil. Danny was rewarded with a warm smile and he said, "I see that you're okay now. Shall we go?"

When I returned to the plant and walked down the corridor, I slowed when I passed Eric's office and glanced inside just to make sure that things were normal between us and that what I thought I had felt emanating from him was simply a figment of my imagination.

Eric had his chin propped up with one hand and was engrossed in a document on his desk, chewing on the end of a pencil – he looked like a student preparing to take an exam. He had apparently heard my steps or felt my glance because, when I was half-way down the hall, he called out to me and asked me to come in.

I came back and sat down in the upholstered chair across from him.

"How was lunch?" he asked.

"Just fine, but I couldn't get him to push for stricter standards."

"That's too bad. We will have to wait for another of our larger clients to do that. Don't worry, it will happen."

"I'm glad you're optimistic."

"I'm always optimistic, even about a meal at an Asian restaurant," he said, smiling in a way that unfortunately proved to me that my imagination was not working overtime.

He was making me uncomfortable and I wanted to leave the room.

"Did I tell you that my son won a silver medal in a swimming competition?" Eric added hurriedly, as a way to keep me from leaving.

I was relieved by the change in direction of the conversation. It's always safer to talk about children. "That's great! Another one to add to his collection."

"Exactly. The wall in his room is almost covered with awards."

"Do you push him to practice?"

He brushed his hand through his wavy hair and the smile almost reached his dark eyes. "They say that behind every successful child athlete are parents who push them to excel and reach their goals."

"I don't know if I would want to pressure mine into bringing home medals."

"And if one of them showed outstanding ability or a particular skill?"

"I don't have to worry about that. They look like regular, normal children. Intelligent, but with no exceptional talents."

"All of them?"

"All three," I made a point of saying, as if he had any inkling that there was another child. In spite of myself, I wondered if 'that' child was normal, intelligent, or blessed with any unique skills. Were the parents who had adopted him the ambitious types, who would want to prove to themselves that their child was special and push him to excel in something? Maybe he had to practice the piano or the violin for long hours every day and wasn't allowed to play or watch television before he had completed his daily quota of scales? Or maybe they made sure that he spent most of his time doing homework so that he could be an excellent student… A moment before I began to resent them, I thought of the opposite: that the child might have been born with a rare gift for music or sport, and it had gone unrecognized or they hadn't supported or encouraged it as if they didn't consider these things to be important. Once again, I felt helpless at my complete ignorance as to his fate.

"Your children are too small; you can't know this early," Eric's voice came to me as if from afar.

I continued the conversation. "That's true, maybe one of them will be the next Mozart or Michael Jordan.

"What about you? What skills do you have that I'm not aware of?"

"I don't know… nothing special. Why do you ask?"

"Just asking. I really don't know much about you."

"What is there to know?" I was startled and, once again, just like yesterday, Daniel saved me by rushing into the room to discuss some work matter.

I went back to the control room and tried to concentrate on my work. Ruth still hadn't called and I kept myself from calling or bothering her with incessant messages.

Chapter 9

Late afternoon on my way home, I joined the snaking highway lined with many, many vehicles and, during the thirty-minute drive, I managed to shake off the vestiges of work – to set aside the matter of standards and the events of the day and tuck them away into separate compartments, to put the springs to bed in a dark room and push away Eric's strange words.

Thoughts of my children and the sweet idea that I would be seeing them soon flooded the void that had been created. I imagined them crowding around my mother, playing and protected from all evil, and was filled with joy. Tears choked me and my eyes misted.

For several years, something had been wrong with my lacrimal system and tears would appear whenever they felt like it, of their own volition. I was unable to control this and it only took one emotional thought or an insignificant, marginal statement for tears to make their appearance, as if drawn from the bottom of my soul.

When Dor would notice tears dropping, he would tell everyone around who might not been aware of it that "Mommy is crying," and Shai would be quick to agree with him, saying, "Mommy is a crybaby." I would laugh at them. The tears would roll down my cheeks and onto my lips, and I could taste the saltiness that did not, in any way, deny the sweetness that filled my heart.

I exchanged my childhood experiences as an only child with a vibrant reality that only quieted when six curious eyes involuntarily succumbed to weariness and closed.

I rang the doorbell. I could hear noises on the other side of the door. Shai and Dor would be fighting to see who reached the door first. Today, Shai beat his big brother and the door opened to reveal the two of them – a smile of victory creasing Shai's face, disappointment on Dor's. But the expressions of exultation and defeat melted away with our three-way hug.

Ya'ara stumbled into the hall, a crumpled cotton cloth diaper pressed to her cheek. She ran to me and, around the rubber pacifier in her mouth, she mumbled, "Me too … me too…"

I made room for her between the boys and it became a four-way hug.

My purse slid off my shoulder and fell onto Shai's back. He wriggled the bag off of him and inadvertently stepped on the edge of his sister's diaper, loosening it from her grip. Ya'ara howled plaintively, "My blankie! My blankie!"

The huddle broke apart. I rescued the blankie and returned it to Ya'ara, hung my purse on the hook next to the door, and removed my coat. The welcoming aroma of the coffee my mother was preparing for us wafted in from the kitchen as if spelling out her greeting. I swung Ya'ara up in my arms, steadied her on my hip, and walked towards the brewing coffee and the warm smile awaiting me there.

We sipped our coffee and talked about trivial things that only had significance within the home and, even that, for only a short time.

Afterward, these trifling matters were stored in the grey cell databases. When I wanted to retrieve something – a piece of information, a memory – it was difficult to find it. Maybe there is a place in the front part of our brain that is separate from the part that stores the grey cells.

"What are you thinking about?" said my mother, rousing me from my musings.

"If they die when there is no more room in the cache memory."

"Who, what died?" She didn't understand.

"Who, what died?" Ya'ara repeated what her grandmother said in a honey-sweet voice.

"No one died, thank God."

"Tank Dod," she said. My mother and I laughed and the little one joined us with cheerful gurgles.

Sometime after my mother and I had said our goodbyes, I heard Gil's special knock – three double knocks, each a second apart. The boys raced for the second time today, reaching for the door handle at the same time, Shai's hand covering Dor's hand. Ya'ara stumbled after them, this time pushing her doll's stroller.

I looked at them, never tiring of the familiar show that took place every day, though each time unique.

Gil's height almost filled the doorway.

I committed the portrait to memory, taking in his short-cut hair, the length that the bristles on his cheeks had grown since his morning shave, and the fatigue hidden behind his warm countenance. He felt my gaze, raised his eyes to me, and threw me a smile. I was flooded with waves of joy. This emotion, which had become a constant in our life's routine, shook itself free and leaped out like a jet of clear water and, once again, he was the boy standing in the doorway of my home the day after the dance party.

But just as it occasionally happens, those nagging, persistent thoughts pushed their way through, uninvited – did that baby, who would be ten years old now, look like his father? Would I one day encounter a mini-Gil striding towards me down the street? In a mall? Somewhere most unexpected?

A tremor shook my being. 'I shouldn't be thinking such thoughts,' I berated myself, and enjoyed the sight of my children in their father's arms where he tickled them just for the delight of hearing their peals of laughter. My joy was diminished by the distress caused by wondering about that child, whom, even in my heart of hearts, I did not dare call 'my eldest.'

Gil's eyes rested on me for a moment and I threw him a quick smile to throw him off the scent of the turmoil within my soul. For as long as we'd been together, we'd always discussed everything in our lives in minute detail: feelings, thoughts, fears, doubts, hopes – but never that.

At times like these I wanted to break this conspiratorial silence but, instead I would go to the bedroom to calm down, the only remedy that seemed to work. It was particularly tough after the children's births, on their birthdays and particularly on his birthday.

I sat down at the edge of the bed and phoned Ruth.

She didn't answer. Just like this morning. What was going on?

I called again. I listened to her ringtone playing 'Strangers in The Night' until the call switched to voicemail.

Was she screening my calls or what? She knew that the day before yesterday had been February 5th, his day.

I called again and, this time, she answered.

"Hi. What's going on? You promised to call."

"Yeah, sorry, I didn't get around to it."

"Did something happen?"

"Just problems at work. I can't concentrate on anything."

"I'm sorry. I hope it works out."

She didn't react.

"In the end, things work out, don't they? Particularly at work."

She sighed. "Yes, in the end. How are you all?"

I told her that everything was ok, and reminded her of the date etched into my heart. "How is he?"

"What? Again?" she asked, knowing exactly who I was referring to. "That's enough. On Shai's birthday I told you that I wouldn't talk with you about this anymore."

"That's right, but he turned ten the day before yesterday. And I only ask you once a year to tell me. Only on his birthday."

"I can't. I don't want to talk about him anymore."

"What am I asking for? Just three words – he is ok. That's all."

She was silent.

"Ruth, please, I can't continue without this. I can only talk about him with you."

"No! It's over!" she shouted.

I shuddered. Something was off in her voice. My beloved aunt, who for long periods of my life had been like a mother to me, did not normally react like this. There was something else in her voice besides anger. Something had happened. My heart said that it was something bad.

"Goodbye, Maya," she said and hung up.

Gil appeared in the doorway, the children hanging on him, squirming and laughing. "Here's mommy. She ran away to the bedroom."

"Is mommy playing hide and seek with us?" Dor asked, enthusiastically.

Gil threw all three of them onto the bed, touched my forehead, and was concerned by my skin pallor.

I said, trying my best to put on a pleasant expression, that I had a headache and was just feeling tired.

Gil ordered the children to stop jumping on the bed and leave the room because mommy wasn't feeling well.

Their voices drifted to the living room.

I laid down on my back, three words running around in my head, harshly, over and over again, "something is wrong."

I don't know how long I lay in that position when I felt Gil's lips hovering over my face, murmuring, "How are you feeling?"

I enjoyed the languor of his caresses, listening to his soft voice telling me that he had finished washing the little ones and had put them to bed, and that it would be no bother at all to wash the bigger girl too. He undressed me tenderly: removing my shoes, peeling off my tight jeans and t-shirt, until all that was left were my bra and underpants. The touch of his hand was calming and dispersed the cloud that had darkened my spirit during the past hour.

Maybe I was imagining it all, I thought to myself, as my bra and panties were swiftly removed and flung bed aside. I was naked, exposed and, through my half-closed eyes, was aware of Gil's frenzied moves, rapidly taking off his clothes. He led me to the bathtub and we both squeezed into it. The warm water calmed me and I gave myself over completely to Gil's soapy hands. I forgot about my children and relinquished all my anxieties for blissful lovemaking, for love. Everything else ceased to exist.
    When we were curled up under the duvet, the world seemed to reclaim its balance. I resolved to abide by what Ruth wanted, to stop pestering her with questions. Not only that; I also made a decision to bury the matter even deeper inside myself and, from then on, sentenced myself to remain calm, inside and out. I would live my life as if it had begun the day after his birth.
    I cuddled up against Gil and felt great relief.

Chapter 10

I was standing at the control room's large window, looking down onto the work floor. I was supposed to inspect the torsion springs department. Moshe Levi – who we called by his full name to differentiate between him and Moshe Cohen, who was only referred to by his first name and who worked next to him – was making small springs for air-conditioners. He preferred not to visit the control room. Due to his exaggerated sense of self-confidence, he observed from alongside the machine because, in his opinion, he was an expert in the use of calipers and, therefore, there was no need for anyone else to inspect the springs that he was manufacturing, especially not me, a novice in the world of springs.

"I couldn't care less what you studied," he protested the first time I asked him to come to the window every two hours. "I have forgotten more than you have ever learned or will ever learn."

I tried to flatter him, to compliment him on his acuity and even belittled myself, and pointed out that my job simply required me to inspect what was automatically being made in his machine. But he was steadfast in his refusal. I lost my patience and asked him some questions with the hope of proving to him that he didn't know everything, but he shot off all the right answers, distancing himself from the window while ignoring my existence, as if I had disappeared into thin air and all that was left of me was an annoying small cloud that left an irritating shadow on his caliper.

After that I took the coward's way out – instead of confronting him, when he would leave the floor to eat breakfast or lunch, I would sneak in and dig into the cartons that he had filled, take out a few of the springs manufactured by him using the machine that he himself operated, and hurried to inspect the pitch between the coils, their length and their tension.

On the days that he filled small orders, I would slip onto the work floor when he went to the restroom and take samples to inspect in the control room. Over and over, I had proof that the springs Moshe Levi manufactured were amazingly precise.

Moshe Levi – who, during the first months, I had mistakenly called Levi Moshe – was short and skinny and at least twenty years older than me. Now, he wiped his hands with a grey cloth, shut down the automated machine and left the room. I looked at his round balding head that, from above, looked like a snowy mountain top. When he had disappeared from sight, I rushed to his station. I dug around in the half-full box, haphazardly taking out a few small silvery springs, hurried to the control room with my booty, and began to inspect them. The pitch between the coils was exact; the length as well, but the diameter of the wire... 0.9 mm! That couldn't be! The customer had ordered 0.8 mm wire. Could Moshe Levi have made a mistake when he selected the wire? I found that difficult to believe.

I changed calipers and asked Elena to check a few springs herself – and the results were the same each time: one-tenth of a millimeter too much and, consequently, the load deviated and was beyond the bounds.

I raised my eyes and saw the arrogant operator striding back to his machine. I rushed to intercept him before he could switch it on again. I stood between him and his machine and told him, as respectfully as I could, that he had made a mistake when selecting the wire. He protested, objecting to the fact that I had taken some springs for inspection behind his back, took the caliper with a confident gesture, and complacently pushed the wire into it. He looked at the number, threw the spring into the pile, took another one, checked it, threw it back, repeating this maneuver over and over again: taking a spring, measuring it, throwing it back. His face reddened. He threw the caliper into his toolbox, lifted the carton in his arms and, with heavy steps, strode to the large recycling bin in the corner of the hall and emptied the box of all the flawed 0.9mm springs that he had just manufactured.

I felt no pleasure from his misfortune, despite all the obstacles he had placed in my way. He returned to his station, lit a cigarette and looked at me as if I was simply smoke that he was exhaling. I told him firmly but in a low voice that mistakes happen and that this was the reason that quality control exists. "From now on, you will come to the window like everyone else. No more concessions."

He didn't reply but his face betrayed his agitation. His professional reputation had been put into question because of a stupid mistake, and a momentary lapse in concentration had pulled the red carpet that he had placed for himself out from under him.

"Well, well, the sheep has come to the wolf, or maybe the Messiah has arrived and the wolf is laying down with the lamb?" Rosenblatt suddenly appeared out of nowhere, spouting his flowery Biblical sayings.

Moshe Levi continued to quietly blow smoke and I said, as aggressively as I could without being overly disrespectful, "The Messiah will arrive when this plant begins to work according to the required level of recognized standards."

"Bless you, Maya. You are in a fighting mood. What happened? You asked for milk and Moshe Levi brought water?"

"Exactly. How did you guess?" I was fed up with both of them, turned my back and returned to the control room.

Later that day, I saw Rosenblatt wandering around the work floor with three guests, two men and one woman. He led them from one machine to the next, tossing out explanations. They were shifting from foot to foot impatiently, hiding yawns. The woman apparently slipped on a spring that had rolled out from one of the stations. She landed on her rear with a cry, right in front of Rosenblatt, who blocked her legs with the heavy safety boots that he always wore when in the plant.

He looked down at her for a moment, puzzled, then quickly came to his senses, bent down and extended his hands to her. She caught them as if they were a lifeline and, for a moment, it seemed as if he would lose his balance and collapse on top of her, but he managed to help her stand up.

An hour later, the three guests left the plant and, just as the heavy door shut behind them, Rosenblatt returned to the station where this had occurred, rebuked the employee who was supposed to sweep springs that fell on the floor, and returned to his office.

Moshe Levi never came to the control window that day – not even once. And so, at the end of the day as I was on my way to stamp my timecard, I stopped next to his machine and told him that as of tomorrow morning, he was to come to the control window on a regular basis. Without waiting for a reaction, I turned on my heel and walked away, slid my magnetic card through the machine and went out into the twilight.

Chapter 11

The thin cover of dusk pulled at my heartstrings, causing me to be more introspective. My anger dissipated. The car seemed to drive itself, allowing my mind free time to wander. It had been three weeks since Ruth had angrily cut off our conversation and although my throat practically closed up every time I thought of the child, I resolved to keep my promise and not pester her. When my parents had us over for Friday night dinner, I tried to feel her out regarding what was happening at work, or in her life, but she sidestepped every question and swiftly changed the subject. She was right and I couldn't blame her – her presence had opened a crack in the restraint that I had imposed upon myself and, had she not avoided me, making certain to never be alone with me, I probably would have abandoned my resolve to stop pestering her about the child.

Today, my father joined in for the afternoon shift and was determined to keep the children occupied. They were completely wild with enthusiasm. They grabbed him and pulled him to their room. He even got down on all fours for a few minutes, despite his paunch which had grown a bit with the years, and pushed a large fire truck around the house. On one side of him, Dor was driving a shiny black and white police car and, on his other side, Shai was pushing a white ambulance sporting a red cross.

"There's no accident," said Dor. "We need an accident."

"Accident! Accident!" Shai cried out.

"There must be a traffic accident," Dor decided.

Shai agreed. "A traffic accident!"

My mother was horrified. "They watch way too much television."

My father got up, straightened his back and, breathing heavily, went back to their room to retrieve a small, battered car and some Lego dolls. Then he organized an accident on the carpet. "Help!" he called out, giving the dolls a voice, and Dor and Shai rushed to the scene with the police car and ambulance.

"I'll be in the kitchen," announced my mother, distancing herself from the scene.

For a while, I was fascinated by their playing but left when the injured were on their way to the hospital and a fire had broken out in the Lego building.

My parents stayed for dinner. We extended the table and took our seats – four adults and three little ones. Gil helped feed Ya'ara while he spoke about the trip he was planning for Shabbat; that is, if it didn't rain, because it really would be a shame to miss the blooming anemones and cyclamens.

"A trip almost every Shabbat? Isn't that a bit too much?" asked my mother. Taking your family on a trek and tiring yourselves out on the only day you have to rest?" she explained.

"Do you really think that it's possible to rest in this house with those three?" my father nodded his head and sided with Gil. He loved our Shabbat trips and often joined us. Sometimes Gil's parents and brothers would join us too.

Gil had fallen in love with the country during his army service and, as far as he was concerned, the children didn't slow him down; moreover, his desire to show them the country's rivers, mountains and valleys only increased his motivation to plan and carry out these outings.

When Dor turned six months, Gil bought a baby sling and put him on his back and, when Shai was born, we bought a similar sling for me. Later, when Dor began walking by himself, Ya'ara took Dor's place in the sling. And so, during their first years, our children saw the country from a height of a meter and a half; thereafter, they conquered the trails with their little legs.

Later that evening, I left the house to coach my girls' basketball team. This was my good deed for the week. My mom had encouraged me to play basketball in an attempt to overcome my sadness and I continued playing even after I had pulled myself out of the depression, even when I was happy with Gil and the children.

When the club approached me and asked if I would volunteer to coach a team of at-risk girls, I agreed willingly. I began working with them a few months after Ya'ara's birth. In the beginning, they were reserved, even cynical, but in time, they fell in love with the game. They kept coming and enjoyed themselves, and I also enjoyed them.

When I got home from practice, Gil was already curled up under the blanket, which covered him up to his eyeballs. He beckoned me to undress and join him right away, despite the fact that I was all sweaty, but I knew I needed a quick shower. Then, refreshed, I didn't bother with a nightdress and joined him under the blanket, right into his waiting arms.

Chapter 12

I woke up in the morning with an inexplicable sense of unease. Gil, on the other hand, was happy and singing in the shower. Suddenly and involuntarily, I was reminded of my last telephone conversation with Ruth. What was different about her? What had happened to cause her to resolutely refuse to say the two words I wanted to hear – 'he's fine.' All sorts of possibilities, each more frightening than the other, made me leap from the bed.

Gil got out of the shower and my eyes followed him as he carefully selected his wardrobe and dressed in front of the mirror. For whom was he primping? I wondered. Once again, for no reason, the fear that he would leave me one day arose, that he would meet someone who was better than me, smarter, someone who had not deceived him in the distant past, who had not pushed him into starting a family at such a young age.

"I have to go to dinner with Hoffman and his wife today. You remember we went to dinner with them to a restaurant at the port a few months ago?"

"Yes, but today I have practice with my girls."

"I know, that's why I'm taking Daria with me, my new intern."

Wow, he had really found a solution fast.

"Anyway, you don't really enjoy these business dinners."

He was right. I filled my mouth with water.

"Will you get a babysitter?" he asked on his way to the door, not forgetting to give me a goodbye kiss and to tell me that he hoped that I have a good day.

Was he giving this Daria special treatment, like Eric was behaving towards me? That thought gnawed away at my already insecure feelings regarding his love and devotion. I continued my morning routine on autopilot. I took the children down to the car, belted them into their car seats, and took my place behind the steering wheel. I glanced in the mirror. I drank in our three sweet ones, shook off the disturbing thoughts and drove away.

I went through my usual morning rounds – checking calibrated measurement instruments, touring the work floor, scrutinizing springs for quality control. Around noontime, I was carrying out a surprise inspection on torsion springs when I noticed a delegation approaching me: Eric, with the three guests who had been there the day before. The woman was walking alongside Eric, seemingly fascinated by his every word, as if he was revealing state secrets. The two men walked behind them.

When they reached the machine where I was examining springs, Eric introduced me, giving my name and position. I had to restrain myself from asking who they were.

I looked at them as they walked away and saw Rosenblatt the father standing in the doorway of his office, following them with his eyes. When they were engrossed in the sharpening department, he looked away, saw me staring at him, and at once turned on his heel and went back into his office.

At one o'clock I went to Eric's office. His eyes were fixed on the computer screen and he was oblivious to the fact that I was there.

"Shall we go to the Asian restaurant?" I asked.

Eric's head jerked up in surprise and he smiled. "When?"

"Now."

"Now?"

I felt that perhaps he regretted what he had said previously and wanted to rescind the offer. "If it's not convenient…"

"Wait. Just a moment. It's very convenient. I'm simply surprised by the about-face? What happened?"

I stayed quiet.

He pushed his chair back and rose to his feet. "Never mind, it's time to go."

The dishes the waiter placed in front of us were amazingly delicious and I cleared my mind of thoughts of Gil and the young intern joining him for dinner. What was happening to me? Gil had never given me a reason to be jealous, to suspect that he was cheating on me. Why was I attributing another man's behavior to him?

At home, I discovered what fine acting skills I had. I behaved as usual, drank coffee with my mother, played with the children, got the neighbor's daughter to babysit them, and changed into sports clothes while Gil changed into a black shirt that complimented him. Then we both left the house, each to his/her own pursuits.

As expected, I returned home before him. I released the neighbors' daughter from her duties, showered, and got into bed wondering when he would return. I went over the small crisis that had occurred during practice – one of the girls became angry because of what one of her friends had said during the game in a moment of excitement, and this had led to an argument between them. I hurried to put an end to the drama, but the warm atmosphere we had during the practice had somewhat chilled. During the time that was left, I tried to lift their spirits by announcing a competition of 'odd shots.'

They cooperated and the bursts of laughter when they made odd and startling shots lessened the tension; and we left practice feeling elated, as usual.

The front door opened and I could hear echoes of conversation, but had to strain to hear the words.

"Your house is so neat. Didn't you say that you have three children?"

Gil laughed. "A few hours ago the living room looked like a battlefield, but Maya put everything away."

"I'm neat too. Obsessively."

Gil offered her a cold drink. "Not wine, we had enough in the restaurant," he said.

Daria – I imagined that's who it was, claimed that she wasn't drunk at all. "Alcohol doesn't affect me."

"It does me… when I drink, I feel like I'm going back in time."

"How far back? To the Middle Ages? Are you a knight in shining armor?"

Gil laughed. "No, to the days when I was in high school, in the army, when I would go to parties."

"So, that would make me your elder and you must respect my wishes: pour me some wine!"

"No, you still have to drive home."

"You're kicking me out already?"

"No. You saved me twice, today. Coming with me and driving me home."

"So, you owe me."

Gil told her that he didn't mind being in debt to the best intern his office had ever had.

"Did you see how Hoffman's wife corrected him all the time?" she said. "She had something to say about everything he said. It was really embarrassing."

"That's their problem," said Gil.

"But it's Hoffman, the office's most important client… property deals in Israel and abroad… to see him acting like a little boy next to his wife … but what do I know about marriage? I'm still single."

"Married or not, part of interning is understanding the client's psyche."

"How did you know that he writes stories for the drawer?" she asked. "I never would have pinned Hoffman for a sensitive writer… Well, I always lose in the game of Truth or Dare."

I decided to come out of the bedroom and join them, just as I was, wearing the sweatsuit I had worn to bed. Daria was wearing a low-cut dress. I scrutinized her: a model's body, on the short side, stylishly cut hair, a smile showing off perfect teeth; as a teenager, she had probably worn braces until her teeth straightened like soldiers standing at attention.

"Did we wake you?" said Gil, surprised.

"No, I hadn't fallen asleep yet."

Gil introduced us and said, "I drank a bit too much at the restaurant so Daria brought me home."

Daria turned to me. "I truly admire you. Playing basketball in the evenings ..."

"I coach the girls' team," I corrected her, "and the truth is that, for me, it's easier than sitting for four hours in a fancy restaurant making chitchat with strangers."

"Actually, I love fancy restaurants."

"I'm sure what your dinner cost could feed an average family for an entire month," I couldn't help myself. Gil knew how I felt about this kind of wasteful spending.

"For Maya, family is most important."

"Gil told me that you coach girls who come from problematic homes," Daria pointed out.

"Today, she coached girls who, thanks to her, touched a basketball probably for the first time in their lives," he said proudly, and then added, "Hoffman and his wife asked about you."

"You explained that I couldn't come, right?"

Daria beat him to it. "He explained it very well, in very flattering terms. Your husband really admires you..."

Before I had a chance to react, she said, "he didn't tell me that you were so beautiful."

I smiled and asked my husband if Daria had a reason for buttering me up.

"Of course, you're the big boss's little woman," he teased me.

I picked up the remote control and turned the television on. "If you don't mind, the news is on; maybe they'll announce whether or not the kindergartens will be on strike tomorrow."

Daria suddenly glanced at her watch and, appearing ill at ease said, "It's late. I think I'll call it a night."

The TV news anchor said:

"*Following the horrendous accident on the Arava road three weeks ago, it was decided to erect a fence along the road where it seems to serve as an animal crossing. As a reminder, the accident occurred when a camel crossed the road and the car crashed into it. A husband and wife, both scientists at the Weizmann Institute, were killed, leaving behind a ten-year-old boy. The family of Amos Grinfeld, senior scientist in genetic engineering, and Gila Grinfeld, who had only recently completed her Ph.D. in molecular chemistry, said that this would only serve as a partial solution and...*"

Gil took the remote from me and turned the television off. "That's enough," he said.

I stared at the dark screen, shocked and dumbfounded. "Their boy is all alone, an orphan..."

"Good night," said Daria, and turned towards the door.

Gil reminded her of their 8 o'clock meeting the next morning. "You'll wake up on time?"

"If you don't trust me, you're welcome to wake me up," she giggled.

After she had left, Gil said that I had not really been very welcoming.

"She exaggerated a bit, don't you think? 'You're welcome to wake me up,' as if you were an available bachelor."

Gil laughed. "Do I hear a hint of jealousy?"

"Not at all," I refuted in a quick, visceral response. "You promised me a donation from Hoffman, remember?"

"Of course I remember. He will gladly pay for the team's uniforms."

"You're unbelievable! You're a magician!"

Gil said, provocatively, that it would cost me, and I begged to put off payment until the next day. I was too tired, but Gil wouldn't give in.

"When will you learn to delay gratification?"

"Tomorrow," he said, laughing, and sat down backwards on a chair, his arms crossed on the back of the chair. I stood behind him and began massaging his shoulders. Gil sighed in pure pleasure.

"She's young, this Daria," I said.

"She didn't go to the army; I understood from her that she had some sort of health problem. That's why she's already an intern."

"An intern who's quite a looker, but not as pretty as me." I massaged his shoulders vigorously.

"Ayyy, not so hard," he complained.

"The couple that was killed in the accident on the Arava road – they were scientists, like my parents … did they say how old the child was?"

"I think they said that he's ten."

I tensed. "Are you sure? That's it, I'm tired." I removed my hands, turned away from him, and picked up my phone.

Gil protested the sudden halt in the massage and asked who I was calling at this hour.

"Ruth." It just slipped out.

"It's almost midnight. Your aunt is probably already deep in dreamland. What's so urgent?"

I didn't reply and listened to the ringing on the other end of the line.

"Okay, then I'm going to shower and wait for you in bed."

Ruth didn't answer. Apparently, her telephone was already on 'silent'.

Chapter 13

I found myself pacing restlessly around the living room. I was too tense and alert to go to sleep. Anyway, Gil had already fallen asleep. I pushed down the little voice inside of me telling me to go to him.

I had no idea how much time had passed or what time it was when Gil came in and approached me, still half-asleep. "Hey, I've been waiting for you… what are you doing here?"

I remained silent, not moving.

He was worried. "Did something happen?"

"I'm thinking about the boy who lost his parents on the Arava road."

Gil didn't understand what I was talking about.

"It's him! It's *his* parents who were killed!"

He was unable to grasp what I was getting at. It's no wonder. This was the first time that I had ever mentioned him to Gil.

"It's the boy in the accident! Don't you get it?"

Gil sighed. He finally understood. His face saddened with pity. "Where is this coming from?"

"He was ten a few weeks ago," I explained.

"Millions of boys are ten years old."

"But he… and Ruth is avoiding me."

Gil didn't understand how Ruth was involved in this, and I confessed to him that several times a year, on his birthday and sometimes on the children's birthdays, I would ask her how he was.

Shocked, Gil was silent and I continued, "and this time, she refuses to tell me."

Gil paced back and forth. "Ruth agreed to this? To tell you how he is? A social worker in the Ministry of Welfare and Social Affairs? What was she thinking?"

"It's my fault," I continued to confess. "From the beginning, I never stopped asking her about him."

"She's crazy. She's not allowed to …"

"I only ask her about him a few times a year."

"Good for you! You really deserve a gold medal for that," he said, with barely repressed anger.

"I didn't ask her what they call him, or the color of his eyes …"

"Such restraint!"

"I can't speak of him with anyone; not even with you. But, once in a while, I have to know if he's okay," I said, trying to justify my actions.

But he reprimanded me. "All these years and you've never told me this! Are we a couple or just two people living in the same house? You've been secretly calling Ruth and asking about him for ten years without my knowledge?"

"I'm sorry."

"I never thought that you would lie to me again, that you'd take revenge on me again."

"Enough, Gil, I didn't do this to get back at you. Think about the boy whose parents were killed!"

"I feel sorry for the boy, that his parents were killed in the accident. What happened to him is terrible. Terrible. Now, I'm going back to sleep."

"And if it's him?" I asked defiantly. "What if they come to us now, to ask if we are willing to take him back…"

Gil cut me off and said that no one would come because it had nothing to do with us.

I couldn't give up. This was not just a coincidence. "Imagine if they were to return him to us."

"Who? This is not the baby you gave up. This is a strange boy that we know nothing about."

"Strange? You and I made him." I shouted.

"It makes no difference. Legally, we have no connection to him. He belongs to his family."

This was the lawyer talking. I was sure of that.

We fell silent for a moment, facing each other. And then I asked, more quietly, "Have you ever thought of him, all these years?"

"Do you really want to have this conversation at three in the morning?" he said, deflecting my question.

"You think about him sometimes, right?" I implored him to tell me, but to no avail. Gil was adamant. "He doesn't exist for me. Not in my heart and not in my mind."

"He does for me! When Dor grimaces, I think, is he also a clown? When Shai asks thousands of questions, I think, maybe he's curious as well… and Ya'ara's dimple… maybe he has one too?"

He was quiet. I felt that my words had reached him. He was still detached, but didn't distance himself from me. I tried again, saying that I did not believe that all this time, all those years, he had never thought about him.

Gil sighed and finally, in a choked voice, admitted that he had thought of him when Dor was born. "When the midwife was so excited that the birth had been relatively easy for a first birth, I suddenly thought: Wow, actually, this is the second time she has given birth…"

"You see? So you do…"

"A few minutes after that, our Dor burst into our lives, I pushed it down and that was it," he cut me off.

"It's too bad that you weren't at *his* birth…" I couldn't help myself.

Gil was silent for a moment, then said in a soft voice. "That's enough, Maya, it happened ten years ago, you can't relive it now, as if you had to make that decision again."

I was silent and he continued. "*I* hope that the baby that you gave up for adoption is living peacefully and happily with the parents that the Ministry of Social Affairs and Welfare picked out for him and *you* think he suffered a tragedy. Why?"

I didn't answer him and he embraced me. "It'll be morning soon. Come to bed. We have another hour to cuddle together. Let's put on the meditation CD, the one that relaxes you… come on."

But I couldn't relax and decided that I would go to Ruth's office in the morning. That way, she wouldn't be able to ignore me.

She was already at her desk when I entered and her face fell after she heard my light knock on her door. Without even giving me a chance to utter one word, she stood up and told me to leave.

I maintained that, once again, she was ignoring me and now she was kicking me out, but she stood her ground. She said she could not and would not talk to me about him again.

"But why?" I cried out, brokenly.

"Because I got mixed up in something," she muttered.

"With what? Tell me what went wrong so that I can understand why you made an about-face on this."

Ruth sighed heavily, sat down and told me that she had arranged an adoption without informing the couple that the birth mother was addicted to drugs and that the baby had undergone a detoxification process.

"Why didn't you say anything?"

"Because I had already offered him to four other couples who got scared and backed out. I was determined to find him a home one way or another," she replied, defiant.

"So you did a good thing, didn't you?" I asked, not understanding.

"I broke the law. I concealed information." She rose, asked me to leave, and waited to accompany me out.

"But what about me?" I refused to give up. "You've been supportive about this all these years; you can't stop now."

"Not only can I, but I must. I'm asking you to leave now. People are due to come in any minute."

But I couldn't leave without knowing. "He's the child whose parents were killed in the accident on the Arava road, isn't he?"

Ruth was dumbfounded. "What? What are you talking about?"

"It was them, wasn't it? Now, a ten-year-old boy is alone in the world."

Adamant, Ruth said that no one is alone in this world. Everyone has a family. She then took hold of my arm and pulled me out of the chair.

But my mouth continued working and I said: "But everything has changed and now he is available…"

"Available!" she snapped. "What is this – a rental apartment that someone moved out of and is now up for grabs?"

"I meant that, without parents, he has returned to the point where we handed him over for adoption," I urged her to go along with me.

She dropped her hold on my arm, embraced me, and said softly, "Maya, don't go there. You have a good life. A wonderful husband. Three children waiting for you at home. Go to them. Let them fill your heart."

Chapter 14

For the past two days Moshe Levi had been coming to the control window each time he operated the automated machine, as per the new requirements, and he continued to come to the window even during the manufacturing stage.

"He's being holier than the Pope," Elena pointed out sarcastically.

Rosenblatt, who often circulated among the workers, couldn't hide his surprise. "You've become a believer, Levi?"

Moshe Levi did not answer, but rather waited quietly while I examined the samples he had brought. The inspection was complete. The springs looked fine, but were not aesthetically pleasing nor were they perfect. After hesitating for a moment, I placed them on the counter and confirmed that the work could continue.

He didn't look any of us in the eye; he just returned to his station with measured steps. My eyes followed him and I wondered what had caused this 180-degree turn in his behavior. Instead of stubbornness and arrogance there was capitulation and acceptance; instead of the perfect springs which he would normally turn out, he was producing acceptable springs which did not inspire awe. Was that the price of conversion? Did this average output and meekness stem from having mistakenly selected the wrong diameter of the wire, or was it due to my reaction to the error?

Later I saw Daniel with the two men and the woman, who looked as if they had become permanent guests of the plant. He was explaining something to them, and the explanation was accompanied by energetic hand gestures. Then he ushered them to the quality control room and, as if Elena and I were either absent or invisible, enthusiastically explained the steps being taken to ensure the quality of the springs.

I was very surprised at the sudden enthusiasm he showed with regard to quality control procedures and went to Eric's office. My curiosity about the three guests who were fussing around my employers, one after the other, overcame any trepidation I felt about being around Eric and my wariness of being alone with him.

His office was empty. I peered through the glass doors of the father's office and saw them sitting on either side of the desk, engaged in what looked like a heated discussion.

"Did you want something?" I heard Daniel's voice behind me.

I turned around to find him and the guests blocking my way.

The door to the office opened and Eric and his father stood in the doorway. I was very embarrassed and quickly maneuvered to get past them,

I walked briskly to the control room and began checking reports that had been piling up, waiting to be processed. When I was finished, I saw that Moshe Levi was staring at his machine, his hands folded in his lap. He wiped his brow and then nervously moved his hand to his thinning hair. I no longer had any doubts – the man was tormented. There is no way that a single mistake calculating the diameter of a wire could have caused this.

I took a caliper and went to him, ostensibly to examine the samples which were being produced.

He ignored what I was doing and didn't even glance at me.

"What's bothering you, Moshe Levi?" I asked him quietly. He was startled and straightened up.

"I can see that you're going through something. You can talk to me about it if you want."

His cheek shuddered and his lips trembled. "Now you've become a psychologist?" he asked sullenly.

"No, but if you want to talk to me about something, stop by my office after four o'clock. I'm planning to stay late today." I turned and returned to my fortress, intentionally skirting Eric's office.

After Elena had left for the day, I made myself a cup of coffee and sat down at the computer. Every once in a while, I would stay late to be able to work in quiet, but today the numbers were running across the screen and I couldn't make any real sense of them.

Thoughts about Ruth's refusal intermixed with my encounter with Moshe Levi. His obvious distress gnawed at me, as did the pain deep inside of me. I raised myself off my chair a bit to look over at his station. He was sitting in front of the machine, staring at the springs that it was spewing out. His body was hunched over, his chin down, his hands lying idle on his legs. I sank back into my chair.

'Why should I care about him?' a small, rebellious voice said inside my head. The man has treated me with disdain, even contempt, from the first day I arrived at the plant; and now, when it seemed to me that his soul was in turmoil, I immediately felt sorry for him and wanted to help with what was bothering him... No, let him deal with it alone, or with his wife, or with his children. At his age, he probably has an adult son or daughter who could lend a listening ear.

That does it, I decided, and returned to the computer. The columns of numbers flickered on the screen and finally produced results. I became immersed in my work but, very soon, the sound of a repressed humming broke my concentration. Moshe Levi was standing on the other side of the control window and three warm springs were lying on the counter. He looked completely at a loss.

My caliper gripped the springs he had brought and I tried to draw his lowered gaze.

"They're alright, but you used to make prettier springs," I threw the words at him mercilessly, trying to pierce his armor, to catch his eye.

When he finally raised his eyes, they were damp. I was struck with pity and softly asked him to come in. He hesitated for a moment, then entered as if he was doing it against his will and sat down in the chair across from my desk. I placed a cup of sweetened black coffee in front of him and pulled over Elena's chair to sit next to him.

"Look, everyone can benefit from talking things out, and it's obvious to me that you are suffering."

He neither confirmed nor denied what I had said.

"If it's something that is connected with work, and I can help…"

He shook his head.

He squirmed in the chair, touched the cup, then pulled his hand away. Finally, he placed his elbows on the desk and covered his eyes with his oily hands.

Hesitatingly, I put a hand on his shoulder. I patted him lightly across the back, but thought better of it and quickly removed my hand, fearing I would embarrass him even more. His shoulders shuddered and silent tears fell. I shrank in my chair, making myself as small as possible. "Moshe," I said, turning to him after several long minutes. "Can I help you with anything?"

"It's something personal," he mumbled.

"That's okay, everything is personal," I said, trying to encourage him. "What happened?"

After another few moments of silence, he removed his hands from his face, revealing tearful, red eyes. "It's my son, he…"

I waited for him to continue, wondering whether to keep silent or say something encouraging.

"He wants to open his adoption file," he said, his voice trembling, then stopped, as if he had said enough and the rest would be obvious to me. He didn't know that he had just thrown a grenade that could destroy me and that soon, a third person might have to come and save us both.

My stunned silence seemed to be an invitation for him to expand on the matter, and he told me in a broken voice that his only son had just turned 18 and now had the legal right to know about his birth parents.

I wasn't sure I wanted to hear more, but it seemed that he needed to pour his heart and he continued. "At the age of 16, he began talking about it, but I thought that it was just a phase, a teenager thing and, with time, it would pass. But a few days ago, he told his mother and me that he had applied to open the file."

My heart stopped and I couldn't get a sound out, but he didn't need any more encouragement from me. From the moment the faucet opened, he couldn't shut it off. I wanted to flee the room and tell him to go back to his machine, but I stayed seated and listened.

"He has everything he needs. We gave him everything. Whatever he asked for and even what he didn't ask for. Where would he find parents like that? All of the overtime hours I worked were for him. For clothes, activities, a safari in Kenya. Everything you could possibly imagine, everything he wanted. He is our life. We received him when he was three days old. He was tiny, with a head full of hair." The memory made him smile, and he grasped at it and the chain of memories that it brought with it, forgetting that I was here, with him.

Then he fell silent, and I thought he had finished, that he would get up and leave, but he wrapped his arms around himself and continued. "It's my fault. Rose was okay. But me… the problem was with me. So we decided to adopt. We waited a long time, three years. We wanted a newborn who would be completely ours. You should have seen the celebration we had at the brit, the baby's circumcision… a gala fit for a prince. And now, he wants to find his biological parents. To hell with biology!!!" He suddenly became angry and, once again, he was the familiar indignant and sullen Moshe Levi. "Who are his parents, anyway? They didn't want him! What is this – a second chance?"

Suddenly, it was as if he had woken from his reverie. He became alarmed, rose and looked at me, embarrassed and, with the reservations of a person who has unintentionally exposed his innermost heart to another, he regretted it and turned his wrath upon the other, an anger which, in fact, he was feeling at himself.

I stood up on trembling legs, still silent. Our gazes met and I finally was able to get out, "maybe it's not 'parents' … maybe there is only a biological mother," and was instantly consumed by the stupidity of my words.

But, in fact, this encouraged him and a spark of appreciation shone in his eyes, as if he had found comfort in the possibility that it was only his wife who had a biological double, and that he would be able to remain the sole father to his son, even if he wasn't from his seed. However, things turned around and for an instant, he seemed ashamed of the relief he was feeling, especially since he was the one who was 'at fault' and, therefore, had no right to reap the rewards.

With that, our discussion ended. He turned away from me and left the quality control room, taking with him the springs that had been inspected, and walked slowly back to his machine.

I watched him and felt my knees give out. How is it that I hadn't considered that one day, in another eight years, my son might try to contact us? That around the time when we'd be celebrating Dor's bar mitzva, a young man who was about to enlist in the army might show up at our door and claim us as his biological parents… I had always thought of the baby I had given up, of the boy, but not of the young man who would come of his own free will.

I sank into Elena's chair, my heart was beating rapidly. We would have to tell the children one day, so that they won't be surprised. Gil would have no choice. In another few years, we would have to talk about him, prepare for his arrival. That is, if that's what he wants. It will depend on him, as Ruth had explained, but I had not listened because, at the time, it seemed so far in the future. I hadn't stopped to appreciate the possibility that he might suddenly spring up, as if from behind a screen, and confront us.

Now he was ten and undoubtedly had already known for several years that the parents who had chosen him and raised him wanted him more than those who had given birth to him. What did he think of us? That we were bad people, troubled people or, God forbid, that we had died?

I shuddered and, all at once, I recalled my last telephone conversation with Ruth. The anger in her voice rang in my ears, as if she had been speaking through a loudspeaker.

I called her and she answered after five rings.

"Ruth, you have to tell me how he is, only how he is."

My aunt sighed and, in a tortured voice, said that she was forbidden from discussing it with me and would never ever speak of this matter with me again, and then hung up.

I couldn't go home and so I called my mother, telling her that I had been held up at work for longer than I thought I would be, and asked if she could stay with the children until Gil arrived.

Chapter 15

It was a restless night. I found it difficult to fall asleep. When the alarm went off, I was grateful for the morning. It had not only put an end to the sleepless night, but the sunrise also brought with it the many chores I had to carry out from the time I opened my eyes until the moment I left the house.

I drove to work in a daze, numb, like a well-programmed robot.

I parked the car and entered the plant. From the window of the control room I could see Moshe Levi laboring to turn the cogwheels of the machine. He raised his eyes for just a moment, our eyes met and we both instantly looked away. After a half hour he arrived at the window with the first samples. His eyes were sunken, red, and had black circles around them.

I returned the springs to him after inspection and his mouth curved into a kind of self-conscious smile before he turned and returned to his station.

Rosenblatt the father's secretary, came and told me that I had been asked to join the meeting in his office.

"The boys are there with him," she said, hurrying me along.

Strange. An unplanned meeting in the 'Ha-Kfitz' plant, where the work flows along known and well-established lines and without any unexpected, urgent matters to discuss…

Eric and Daniel were sitting at the simple rectangular table in front of a filing cabinet and brown Formica office furniture that had once been the height of fashion. At the head of the table sat their father in a well-worn executive armchair.

Six dark almost-identical eyes stared at me, but I only saw one pair. Eric was smiling at me. I sat down in the only unoccupied chair, across from the father, and concentrated on looking only at him.

"What happened to your beautiful eyes, Maya, Gil's wife?" he gushed. "Which child kept you from sleeping?"

The bubble of pain inside of me suddenly burst, and tears choked me.

"Father, leave her alone," said Eric, coming to my rescue.

"What happened? To what do we owe the honor of this urgent meeting?" Daniel cut off the chitchat impatiently.

Eric, elated, turned from me and announced, "We received a letter from 'Hydroline.' They have received a large order from the United States, with the stipulation that all the components must comply with the new standards."

Daniel was resoundingly silent. A large order from Hydroline, a long-time and important client.

"Since we have been putting off the inevitable, we must act quickly now. We're lucky that Maya has already begun working on the standards procedures despite your objections," Eric pointed out.

I wanted to rejoice, to take pride in my convictions, but the child refused to make room for that, neither in my heart nor in my head.

I returned to the control room. Elena had stamped her time card and was leaving. Eric came to see if I was alright. He said that I looked somewhat tense before, during the meeting. I didn't have a chance to answer him as, right at that moment, the mysterious guests – the two men and the woman – entered the work floor.

"Who are those people?" I asked him.

"They have a springs plant in Germany and they are interested in investing in an Israeli company," he answered curtly.

"To go into a partnership with them?"

"Apparently. Daniel contacted them."

"Daniel?"

"Yes, and Father was enthusiastic at the prospect of expanding the plant, of adding another department."

"And you?"

"I don't know. First, I want to be sure of their intentions," he said and gestured with his head as if towards the other three.

Slowly, the plant emptied of workers and I sat at the computer trying to catch up on some work. My mother was surprised when I informed her that I would be late, again. I don't usually forego fun time with the children but, this time, Hydroline had provided me with a real reason to stay behind in the quality control room.

Moshe Levi knocked on the counter hesitantly and asked permission to enter.

"Would you be willing to be my psychologist?" he asked, hesitantly, and sat down in the empty chair without waiting for a reply.

He squirmed on the chair a bit before opening up and telling me that his son had spoken with his biological mother on the phone and had made a date to meet her the next day at a café in Tel Aviv.

Once again, he sounded infuriated. "Have you ever heard of such a thing? To meet the woman who gave birth to you 18 years ago, in a café? What will they talk about? Will she apologize for giving him up? Will she tell him a heart-wrenching story about why she had to give him up? Will she be curious to see if he resembles her, or someone in her family? What good will it do?"

"What about the father?" I asked.

"At this point, there is no father." His voice revealed the relief he felt in spite of himself. "There was no father's name in the file. Maybe she'll tell him something tomorrow," he retreated, fearfully.

At 7 p.m., I was still trying to tie up loose ends at work, but that was mainly because focusing on the computer screen gave me an excuse to stave off life for a while. Eric came to my office to point out that we were the only two people left in the plant. The blood rushed to my head. I shut down the screen and stood up, a bit unsteady on my feet. He grabbed me and I tried to avoid his support, fearing that I would fall apart in his arms in a moment.

"For some reason, you looked as if you needed help," he said quietly.

"You want to help me? Maybe be my psychologist?" I asked with a laugh, and imagined a tower of amateur psychologists à la 'Yertle the Turtle,' where each one listens to the troubles of the one below.

"Psychologist?" he said, surprised. "All I wanted to do was help you."

"Psychologists don't help?" I made it more difficult for him.

"I hope they do."

"Does your wife help everyone she listens to?" I asked, bringing her in the picture, thus reminding him of her existence. Reminding myself.

"I'm sure that she does her best."

"Does she tell you about her conversations with patients?"

"Not at all. You know that there is a matter of confidentiality."

"On the other hand, you can talk to her about everything that happens here, the clients, the employees..."

"Why would she be interested? She has to deal with enough people and their troubles every day."

"Maybe she could give you her professional opinion regarding someone you might feel is problematic."

"You really think so? That wouldn't be very professional on her part, and I wouldn't burden her with that."

"Have you spoken to her about me?" My tongue spoke as if it had a life of its own.

"The truth is, I did," he said, surprising me. "I told her about your determination to introduce standards to the company."

"Ah, that's good. Well, bye, see you," I said on my way out of the control room. I stamped my time card and opened the door. How had I not heard the pouring rain? My umbrella was in the car. That's usually the way it went – I didn't have it with me when

I needed it most – but then Eric appeared behind me with a huge black umbrella that protected us both. "The mule and the jackass already went home?" I asked as we got to my car.

"Who?"

"Your father and brother."

He stared at me for a moment and burst out in infectious laughter, drawing me hesitantly into the laughter. Then his cellphone rang and he and his umbrella turned and walked away from me leaving me standing there, exposed.

Instead of rushing into my car, I stood there, lifted my head and surrendered to the downpour. I was drenched, my body shuddered and, I finally allowed myself to cry, using heaven's tears as a cover.

Chapter 16

Shai was riding his toy horse around the house shouting, "Mommy's crying, mommy's crying..."
"Mommy's a crybaby, mommy's a crybaby!" Dor chimed in. He was busy moving his yellow bulldozer along the floor.
"Daddy, you *cwying?*" asked Ya'ara, hugging her doll closer to her. "Ya'ara also *cwy*. Dolly also *cwy*."
But only Mommy was crying, and Daddy threw her a worried look while he cut vegetables for the salad and she sliced the bread, set the table and slipped away to take a shower.
The hot water scorched my skin but did not warm me up. I was still shaking after I had dried myself off and put on my sweatsuit, but forced myself to help Gil put the clean children to bed. I even managed to keep from crying long enough to tell them a story.
I turned on the electric spiral heater in the living room and sank into an armchair. Worries about the child's fate overshadowed everything, like a solar eclipse where the moon casts a shadow upon the earth and blocks the sun's rays from getting through.
Good strong hands massaged the nape of my neck, messing up my hair.
"What will happen to the child? Maybe they are searching for his biological parents?" I flung the words at him what has been pecking away at my brain non-stop.
He took his hands away.
"We have to take him back."
"Why? Because you have decided that he is ours?"
"I am certain of it."

Gil moved away from me. "Even if what you have fabricated in your mind is correct – it's impossible. The law is against us."

"How do you know? You specialize in contracts," I protested.

He wasn't daunted. "Everything about this is against the law – the fact that Ruth gave you information, and the fact that… you know what? Wait." He went and got his laptop, opened it, scrolled down and began reading: "Adoption law: in a closed adoption, contact between the parent and the child is completely severed and the parent is not entitled to receive any information about the child."

"Wait a minute, there are 'open' adoptions?" I cut him off.

Gil said there was, indeed, and continued reading: "The official term is 'post-adoption contact agreement' where contact between the minor, his or her adoptive family and the biological parents are not severed after the child's adoption has been finalized."

I broke in once more, "So why, with us…"

He did not wait for me to complete my sentence and continued, emphatically stating, "because an open adoption is considered an exception and the courts permit it only in rare cases and under exceptional circumstances. When you handed the baby over for adoption, there were no exceptional circumstances."

"I was never told that such a possibility existed," I complained.

"Because it wasn't possible. Listen, 'experts are unanimous in concluding that a complete separation from the natural parents is in the best interest of the child in order to avoid potential emotional complications.' That's it. I have nothing to add. The law speaks for itself."

"The law," I said, frustrated. "Don't be an attorney now. Be a father."

"I am as much a father as possible. In my wildest dreams, I never thought that, at my age, I would already be father of three."

"Four. You have four children," I didn't give up.

"But we made up for it, didn't we?" he asked, quietly.

"That's what you call this?" I said, raising my voice.

"Yes. Getting married and having three children in less than six years, all while studying and working? That didn't just happen, you know."

"I can't give up on him."

"Why do you insist on pursuing this? We have a good family, wonderful children, why can't you be satisfied with that?" he insisted on knowing.

"Because he's been dwelling inside of me from the moment they took him..."

He didn't react.

"All these years, we've been living as if it hadn't happened."

"So our whole life together has been one big sham?"

I was quiet. I wanted to deny it but my tongue wouldn't cooperate.

"Are you aware of what you are doing to us because of a child that you are imagining is ours?"

"He's ours just as much as Dor, Shai and Ya'ara are. Can you imagine a situation in which we'd ever give them up? Hand them over to other people?" Now he was the one who was silent. "You must think that I've gone crazy."

He didn't say anything but looked so demoralized.

"Don't worry, I won't sink into a depression," I promised, hoping that I was right.

He left the room. I followed him to the kitchen and watched as he filled the electric kettle with water, poured the water with a bit too much force and pushed the 'on' button as if he was practicing karate. He practically slammed the cup down on the counter and stirred the granulated coffee and the sugar with the spoon as if he was mixing concrete. I had no doubt that Gil wouldn't hesitate to challenge me to a battle.

Chapter 17

The next day I wouldn't allow myself to take a break. I sat at my desk in front of the computer, went to the control window, wandered around the machines, followed up on the work of the operators. It was clear to me that I had to see this project through. My personal problems were of no interest to Hydroline and Moshe Levi's problems did not interest me today. I could see that he was trying to catch my gaze, waiting for an opportunity to talk to me. His cheeks were pallid and his eyes sunken, with dark, half-moon bags under them.

He knocked on the door of the control room at noon, just as Elena went out for lunch. He sat down heavily in the chair, threw me a pathetic look and, without skipping a beat, began pouring his heart out to me, as if our two conversations had been enough to turn me into his confidant. "He liked her. She's nice. He believed her story, he's not angry with her for giving him up for adoption. It wasn't her fault. Someone took advantage of her when she was 17 and abandoned her, pregnant. She had no choice. Her parents pressured her into giving him up for adoption."

He rose from the chair and began wandering around the room as if I wasn't there. As far as he was concerned, I was simply an ear that listened.

"She wants to meet us. To come and see us."

"Come to your home?" The ear had a mouth and even spoke.

"Yes. Have you ever heard of anything like that? She has a lot of nerve." After a short silence, he added, "She has no family. She was married once and got divorced after six months, and that was that."

"She has no other children?"

"No – only our boy!" he shouted. It was a good thing that everyone was out for lunch.

"Moshe, calm down," I went to him and held his hand. "Sit down. I'll make you some coffee."

He obeyed and, in despair, sat back down in the chair. "She waited 18 years for him to look for her. He seems pleased. He told us about her, smiling like a fool."

I gave him a cup of coffee. He stared at it and said, "She'll take our son away, I can feel it. She'll steal him from us in broad daylight."

I was helpless, standing in front of him as he cried, his shoulders shaking. I had no words of comfort. Could it be that during those long, lonely years, she had dreamed of being reunited with the only child she had ever had and, now, after he had come looking for her, would do anything to turn back time?

Something at the control window caught my attention. Rosenblatt and Daniel were coming. I was embarrassed when the door opened and they entered.

"Levi, I see that you are carrying on an affair with the head of our Quality Control department," said Daniel mockingly.

Moshe Levi jumped up from the chair and stood, confused. He had been so engrossed in his troubles that he had not noticed their entrance.

"But to cry over her? That's going a bit overboard, isn't it?"

Moshe Levi did not reply, but fled the room without looking back.

"You are heartless," I said to Daniel.

"As a matter of fact, I had my heart checked and it turns out that it is where it's supposed to be and is ticking away like a clock."

"So you have no soul."

"What's that?"

"I don't know, but I'm sure that it can't be mapped."

Elena came in and father and son began talking about the reason for their visit: they wanted to know when we would be receiving the approval for complying with the required standards. All of a sudden, after all my pleading, this was finally an important issue? I was quite upset but buried my feelings while I explained to them that my work on the procedures manual was coming along nicely, but I still needed a few days before we'd be ready for representatives of the Standards Institute to come and examine it. They took their leave, but not before the father complimented Elena with a line from King Solomon's Song of Songs, which the son translated as: "He says that you have pretty legs."

Elena smiled, pleased, and then looked at me. "Did something happen? Your eyes are red. Have you been crying?" she asked innocently, adding, "you've been so serious the last few days."

I wanted to share my thoughts with her but the words stuck in my throat. Suddenly I felt lonely, despite my two most important pursuits in life – my family and my work – and asked myself if Elena had any friends, male or female, in her life, especially as she had come to the country from Ukraine by herself, leaving her family behind in Kiev.

I shrugged it off and she went to make coffee.

My thoughts went to Gil's and my social life, which basically came down to his office events that we were obliged to attend. Sometimes we'd have his two buddies from the army over, or my friend, Sharon, all three still single.

Maybe Gil missed being in touch with friends, maybe he would like to go out and have fun more often, maybe he missed the single life which had been cut short when we were reunited seven years ago outside basketball practice? No, I calmed myself, he loves our life. The family we created. Me.

"I lead a serially monogamous life," said Sharon, describing her relationships with men. She had found that definition, which I thought was spot on, in a handbook for singles: a serial monogamist is a person who maintains long-time, monogamous, romantic relationships and who, when one comes to an end for whatever reason, starts a new serious, long-term relationship, and so on and so forth.

I found it difficult to understand. "How can you fall in love, create a deep connection, and then ruin it all – over and over again?"

"See? I am a serial monogamist!" she said to me, laughing.

Suddenly I missed her, her open-mindedness, and how easy she was to talk with. I wanted to tell her everything, with the hopes that she would understand and support me.

Elena placed a cup of coffee in front of me. "Thank you. I didn't sleep all night," I said.

"Well, with three children, that's no surprise."

A shiver shot through me and I almost opened my mouth to tell her about the fourth child, but she went to the window to deal with Moshe Levi, who was standing on the other side, samples in hand.

"You didn't sleep all night, either?" she asked him, while inspecting the diameter of the springs.

He looked over at me and our eyes locked. My self-consciousness was squirming inside of me. I was careful to keep our relationship one-sided, keeping my secret hidden, even though it was a scenario which was so similar to his.

Chapter 18

In the evening after the children had been put to bed and were sleeping, I met up with Sharon in a café and poured my heart out. Contrary to what I had thought and hoped would happen, she sided with Gil.

"But why? Why should the child be punished because we put him up for adoption?" I protested in despair.

"You mean why should you be punished."

"I thought that you, of all people, would understand me."

"I understand. I simply don't agree with you."

We drank our ginger tea with lemon in silence. An overwhelming feeling of loneliness hit me once again and now it weighed on me even more, with a dollop of sadness.

"Sweetie, why don't you come with me to yoga?" Sharon asked, her willowy frame built as if it had adapted itself to various yoga positions. I imagined her giving herself over to guided meditation after the physical exercises, and then happily sharing the wondrous experience with her friends in the group, just as she was sharing them with me now.

I didn't react.

"I think that yoga would calm you. It offers a different perspective," she said, not giving up.

If only yoga could solve my problems, but I didn't think that any Eastern philosophy could provide me with another outlook for what was eating away at me.

I slipped into the bed, careful not to wake Gil, but he stretched out his arm and pulled me to him. We lay entwined, our faces close.

We didn't talk. His hand stroked my hair and wiped the tears from my cheeks. When I hesitantly touched his face, my fingers found that his eyes were wet too. I put my lips close to his, kissed his mouth, and then the tears that I had been holding back burst out, uncontrolled.

Gil pressed me close to him, hard, his body shuddering from crying. His heavy sobbing increased the pain that was twisting inside of me. I tortured myself with a feeling of guilt.

I had to let go, I decided once again, just like I had two weeks before. I have to let the child live his life. Come to terms with the fact that he is no longer in my life.

A small hand touched my shoulder. Shai was standing next to our bed. Instinctively, I pulled the cord of the night light and the glow illuminated our faces, both mine and Gil's.

"Why is Daddy crying?" he said, his small voice fearful.

"Sometimes, daddies cry too," Gil replied.

"But why?"

"When something hurts."

"Did you get hurt?" came the obvious question.

"No. My heart hurts."

"Does Mommy's heart hurt too?" he continued.

I said that it did, and he looked at the both of us suspiciously. He then had a brilliant idea: he would kiss mommy and daddy's hearts and the pain would go away. He checked where our hearts were and lavished noisy kisses on our chests.

Chapter 19

For the next two days I emptied my head and heart of all external thoughts and immersed myself completely in the procedures required to enable the plant to receive the long-awaited standards approval. The inspection from the Standards Institute was set for the week after next and I asked Eric to ensure that the whole factory would be scrubbed thoroughly. "Don't worry, the plant will shine like my mother's house after she cleans it again, from top to bottom, when it is already spotless," he promised.

Moshe Levi did not come to work and I was grateful for that. In his absence, it was easier for me to stick to my decision to drop the matter of the boy but, when Tuesday morning came around, there he was, at his station as usual, throwing me looks that revealed his deep distress and I was, once again, plunged into the darkness. I waited impatiently for Elena's lunch break. He entered the room just after she left, looking shorter and thinner than ever. Some white hairs had appeared on his bald head. Perhaps I hadn't noticed them before, or maybe they were the result of the fear and pain he had been going through over the past week.

Moshe Levi was quiet, wringing his hands together restively. Finally in a hollow voice, he said: "So, she came over, invaded the house, kissed up to Rose, complimented her on her cooking, on her taste in decorating. She won her over with that nonsense."

"Is she a nice woman?"

"Who cares if she's nice or not? She took over. First the boy, and now Rose. That's it, she's part of the family now."

"But the boy... is he happy?" I dared ask.

"Happy? He's confused, that's for sure."

"Why are you so against this?"

The landline telephone rang before he had a chance to answer; on the other end was a client who had much to say. In the meantime, Elena returned and Moshe Levi left and, when I was finally able to end the conversation, there was a line at the window counter and I joined Elena to help inspect the springs.

Over the next few days, there was a noticeable increase in activity. Everyone was occupied with cleaning the plant, paying particular attention to the work floor, around the machines and the furnaces and to the storeroom. Everything possible was being done to ensure the plant was ready to comply with the strict standards. They even brought in a gardener to liven up the dull landscaping outside. He planted large flowering bushes next to the entrance and placed large pots with beautiful green plants in the offices. Eric ignored his brother's cynical comments about the plants and his attempts to beautify the place. "What good will this do? If everything is fine, then..."

This time, his father cut him off. "If there are flowers at the entrance of the plant, it is a sign that our plant is blooming and that it is dependable."

"To me, it looks like play-acting, as if we are trying to ingratiate ourselves," Daniel continued.

I looked at him. Outwardly, he resembled his brother so much but his behavior and temperament were so different.

"Why are you so negative all the time?" I asked him.

Silence. Rosenblatt and his two sons looked at me and were so quiet that I became suspicious that there was some underlying reason for his being so dismissive about every change made for the betterment of the plant. Could they be hiding something from me?

"Because I feel like it," he grumbled and went into his office.

Eric and I were left standing next to the philodendron, which had been carefully grown and cared for in the nursery and was now spreading its shiny leaves over the edge of the large planter, its new home.

Eric shot me an embarrassed look and he, too, went into his office.

In the afternoon, while my mother and I were drinking coffee in the kitchen, she told me that Ruth had sounded troubled and worried lately, but claimed that nothing was wrong. "Do you call her sometimes?" she asked and suggested that I invite her over more often. "You know that she loves the children. Have her enjoy a nice family dinner with you."

I nodded, not saying a word.

Gil sent me a message saying that he would be a little late. He was planning on spending time in the press archives to look for something in the database.

He was crazy about old newspapers. To this day, the shelves in his old room in his parents' house were filled with volumes of children's magazines. Whenever we would go there he would look through them with the children. Every time he needed something related to work, he would jump at the opportunity to visit the municipal library and browse through volumes of old daily newspapers or periodicals stored in the archives.

He arrived home as Shai and Dor were splashing around in the bath. He leaned over the bathtub and helped the ducks and boats sail through the foamy water, but his mind seemed to be far away and preoccupied.

"How was work?" he asked me much later, when we were both staring at the small screen, as if he was simply fulfilling his obligation by feigning interest in what kind of a day I had had.

"Okay. The inspection by the Standards Institute is in two days. Keep your fingers crossed for me."

After another short silence, I asked him what he had been looking for in the press archives, and he told me about an article that had been published the previous year in the financial section of the Ha-Aretz newspaper that might assist him in a lawsuit for his client, a building contractor.

"Who's right?"

"As usual, there are two sides to everything."

"If you could choose, which of them would you want to defend?"

"You know that I prefer to defend the underdog."

"But, in this case, the contractor is probably not the weaker one."

"Maya, really," he became impatient. "This is a question that I already answered for you, and myself, during my first year of internship. I represent my clients to the best of my ability and am an officer of the legal system. When a client comes to me, I base my opinion on the law and look for precedents that might be in his favor."

"Back to the law," I point out.

"One never abandons it."

I had ruined the moment with my questions and, if he had been open to an intimate conversation before, he had clammed up now.

Chapter 20

The next day Elena greeted me with a question. "What are you planning on wearing tomorrow?" I answered that I hadn't thought about it.

She couldn't understand how I could not have given thought to this issue. "Aren't you tired of wearing jeans and a blouse?" She showed me an ad in her phone about a sale of flattering jeans. "At least buy a new pair of jeans!"

I feigned interest at the selection and looked through photographs of blue jeans and black jeans, one after the other. The music station on her phone switched from music to the news. There had been a traffic accident. A motorcyclist had skidded on a spill from an oil tanker. Suddenly I felt my blood pressure rising. My lungs rebelled and breathing became difficult.

I got up and handed her phone back to her. "Elena, can you manage alone? I forgot that I have to go home early today."

"You're going out to buy something, right?" she said, smiling, and winked at me.

I made an effort to smile back at her and hurried to leave.

Outside, the sky was blue. A crisp and clear winter day. I took off my sweater, started the car and drove towards the shore. I found parking near the boardwalk, sat on a bench, and began surfing the internet for details about that accident. I remembered the date I had heard about it on the news and searched Google. I found them. "A man and his wife were killed in a traffic accident on the Arava road. They left behind a ten-year-old boy who had stayed at home with his grandparents."

I stared at the photograph of the victims. They looked to be in their forties, looking straight at the camera, full of life.

When I finally arrived home, the streetlights were already on.

The door to our house opened on my first knock. Gil looked worried. "It took you so long to buy a pair of jeans?"

What are you talking about, I wondered to myself, and headed to the bedroom.

"What did you buy?" he said, following me.

"I didn't buy anything."

"So where were you?" he asked, suspicious.

"Around."

He gave me a sharp look. I shuddered. This was probably the terrifying look he used when questioning someone on the witness stand.

I went to the children's room, hovered over the beds, and took in the aroma of shampooed hair and clean sheets, inhaling Dor and Shai's sweet breath and the combined smell of milk and rubber emanating from Ya'ara's mouth.

I sent him the article I'd found, heard the ring confirming that he had received the message and searched his expression as he read it.

"Two scientists from the Weizmann Institute in Rehovot, Amos and Gila Grinfeld, were killed late afternoon yesterday when their car overturned on the Arava Road after colliding with a stray camel. Behind them was a bus filled with tourists which was forced to make a sharp left turn but was able to come to a stop just a few meters from them. The driver immediately called for assistance; unfortunately, the paramedics who arrived on site could only confirm their deaths. The bus driver said that the driver of the car had not been driving too fast for that road. This was not the first instance of a fatal car crash on the Arava road caused by wildlife unexpectedly crossing.

The Grinfelds left behind a ten-year-old son who had remained with his grandparents. The Weizmann Institute stated that Amos Grinfeld had worked in the field of genetic engineering and Gila Grinfeld had recently completed her doctoral degree in molecular chemistry. Their tragic deaths cut off promising careers."

The couple could be seen smiling in the photo. These were the people who had diapered the baby to whom I had given birth, had fed him baby formula from a bottle, hugged him, kissed him and breathed in his scent, encouraged him when he took his first step. They were the ones that he had called Mommy and Daddy.

The child was probably smart, found microscopes exciting, and was enrolled in classes for gifted children who loved science.

Gil finally raised his eyes.

"You are sending me this article to back your theory, based on the fact that Ruth refused to give you answers."

He went to shower and came back dry and naked. He stood in front of the dresser and leaned over to take underpants out of the drawer.

I wanted to forget everything, to move closer to him and embrace his familiar, beautiful body, to rid myself of this craziness that wouldn't let up but instead, I remained rooted in place.

That night he slept with his back to me. My hand was close but I didn't dare touch him. Out of nowhere arose that familiar, niggling fear that he would leave me. That he would fall in love with and prefer someone more easy-going, without a painful past, over me. I wished I could be like that. If only my thoughts of the boy we had lost didn't weigh upon me so heavily, I thought, and became frightened.

For over an hour I waited for sleep to come, but in vain, and so I got out of bed and went into the living room. My thoughts wandered to things that Sharon had told me after one of her yoga lessons, something about the soul choosing its next parents for itself during reincarnation. If that was true, then maybe the boy's soul had regretted choosing me and Gil? Had it had pushed me to hand him over to other, better parents? Sharon also told me that everyone has a purpose in life, and that we all dedicate some part ourselves to searching for that purpose.

Maybe because of the child's purpose we were chosen to be the hosts for a soul that was to be held in deposit for two scientists who were unable to have children, for them to fulfill their own purpose during that chapter of its life? For example, to be able to invent something so great that it would bring about a revolutionary change in the world.

There was something calming in that thought and I enjoyed it for some time, imagining the future: the young man would finish his studies in medical research with honors, and we – his parents and siblings – would be sitting in the audience, proudly applauding. Our proud parents would be sitting next to us, and beside them, an older man and woman – the child's grandparents – also beaming with pride. My heart would overflow with love for all my children, for Gil, for my parents and for the child's grandparents, who had raised him until he reached 18.

But this cheery image ended abruptly when a wave of reality sank my imaginary vessel. Eight years would have to pass before I would be able to grab this dream by its tail.

And even then, only if the boy wanted it.

Chapter 21

In the morning I was curled up in the space vacated by Gil. He had already set up the ironing board in the corner of the bedroom and placed a white shirt upon it. The hot iron made hissing noises when the distilled water hit the material.

My eyes wandered to the ceiling and I was surprised to discover very small, almost imperceptible cracks in it, like scouts that were trying to explore how they could carry out their invasion. Ya'ara, lying next to me, asked what was I looking at and I explained it to her but, the more I tried to direct her gaze, the harder it was for her to see the cracks and, in the end, she became upset and burst into tears.

Gil raised his eyes to the ceiling to see what all the fuss was about. He became distracted and his hand involuntarily stopped moving the iron back and forth on the shirt. When he lowered his gaze, he saw and could smell the brown outline of the iron on the burned, white fabric and let out a heavy sigh.

Later, Rosenblatt passed me in the corridor and wished me a jolly good morning. Daniel, who appeared behind him as if he was his bodyguard, observed, "You should get a good night's sleep if you intend to take this plant into the twenty-first century."

This time I didn't hold back. "Can you tell me what I did to you for you treat me like an enemy?"

He blushed and his mouth opened and closed like a fish out of water, then he turned on his heel and left.

"What's the matter with him?" I asked his father, who was staring at his son's back with a frozen expression. He turned away from me without answering.

"Is everything ready?" Eric said, approaching. He looked tense.

Elena came out of the quality control room and, after calling out a quick "good morning," crossed the work floor on her way to the automated machine.

"We're ready," I mumbled. Certainly Elena was ready, I thought, smiling to myself. It looked as if the eyes of all the employees were fixed on her, openly or furtively. She was wearing a snug black dress that hugged her shapely body and tight leopard-leather boots that encased her seemingly endless legs. A short grey angora sweater completed her look and was a fitting backdrop for her dramatically made-up eyes and her lips that sported a golden-brown lipstick. She looked amazing and I felt like the ugly duckling.

It was a good thing that I had pulled the white collar of my blouse out from under the green sweater that I had selected without too much thought. At least it gave me a bit of a festive touch.

"We're ready," I repeated and entered my kingdom.

The Quality Control department was unusually tidy, and there was no doubt that all the credit should go to Elena.

She came back in and looked at me critically.

"You don't look good," she pointed out emphatically. "Will you agree to put on a bit of makeup?" Her suggestion embarrassed me and even made me a bit defensive. "Why do we have to make ourselves pretty for the inspectors? What is this, a circus?"

"If you were a man, you would shave for the Standards Institute, wouldn't you?"

Her reasoning amused me and I gave in. "You've convinced me, I'll let you make me up for the Institute."

She shut the blinds, took makeup out of her purse and began working on my face. She emphasized my eyelashes, became excited from how the black line she drew on my lower lids brought out the greenish-brown of my eyes, brushed blush on my cheeks and dotted my lips with lipstick. These few unexpected moments of intimacy connected us. "Now, look in the mirror. Can you see the difference?"

A strange face looked back at me from her small compact mirror and, for some reason, I felt comfortable with the outcome. "But you have to sleep at night. Make your husband get up for the children," she added.

The door opened and Eric peeked in. "They're coming," he said. When he saw the new me, he was taken aback and gave me a shy smile. "It suits you."

The Standards Institute had sent two of their inspectors, a man and a woman. The man's eyes were instantly focused on Elena's body moving towards them, as if drawn to it by magical threads; but his partner's eyes only gave it a short once-over. She was carrying and referring to the procedures manual, occasionally mumbling or asking for explanations. The tense atmosphere was somewhat alleviated when the hot coffee and fresh pastries were served. The two representatives from the Institute inspected the dozens of sections of the book, one after the other. They took turns coming to the window or to one of the automated machines, and closely followed the application of various standards during the spring-manufacturing process.

No one was more surprised than me that I managed to focus on them and what they were saying, to answer all of their questions and coherently explain the process. After examining the tracking procedure which followed how a disqualification was corrected, they seemed to be satisfied with the results. The grade of 'satisfactory' was given after every inspection, without even one 'needs improvement.'

Elena smiled at me over the bent heads, and I returned her smile. For the first time in many days, I was able to genuinely enjoy something. When Moshe Levi came to the window holding sample springs for ballpoint pens, outwardly, he looked as he normally did: cleanshaven and his hair combed. However, he seemed detached and was expressionless; I averted my eyes so that he would not ruin my reveling in success.

Everything I had hoped for from the moment I had first entered this plant, was about to come true. Two more sections and victory was at hand. And indeed, the female inspector jotted down the word 'satisfactory' twice more and shed her stern look. "You did very good work," she complimented me.

My eyes met Eric's and I gave him a 'thumbs up.' He smiled broadly and returned the gesture.

I accompanied the inspectors to his office and we took our seats around the table, raising glasses and enjoying burekas and more pastries.

When the two inspectors had left the plant, high on carbohydrates and sugar, I couldn't help myself and once again said to Daniel that I couldn't understand why he wasn't sharing in the joy.

"You don't have to understand."

But I wouldn't give up. "Why not? I think I have a right to know why you are still disappointed, even after we successfully passed the standards test."

Rosenblatt and Eric were squirming in their chairs, uncomfortable.

"What right?" he blurted out, contemptuously.

"Even your father and brother want to know why you are always such a sourpuss!"

He let out a bitter laugh and said, angrily, "They know very well why. They stick with these damn springs and are not willing to try anything new."

"I don't understand, today…"

"What is there for you to understand? You screwed me. Who asked you to introduce these rotten standards?" He had lost control. "Now this horrible plant will live forever!"

I stared at him, stunned. I was beginning to catch on.

Eric was about to say something, but it was impossible to sidetrack Daniel from his diatribe. "You have the right to know? So, here it is! We could have sold it. We had some serious buyers!

We would have been able to invest the money in something new. In hi-tech! In a start-up! Make a fistful of money!" his voice rose into a shout.

"That's enough!" Eric said with pent-up rage.

The father struck the desk with his fist and said to Daniel, not mincing his words. "No one is forcing you to stay here!"

The room was too small to contain the oppressive silence that ensued.

For a moment, Daniel stood before the three of us like an animal caught in bright headlights and then said, in a sulky voice, "Okay, I don't belong here anymore, find yourself a new production manager," and slammed the door behind him as he left.

I stared at the three burekas that looked so lonely on the plate and, all of a sudden, everything bothered me – my eyes burned from the makeup, the collar of my blouse was scratching my neck, and I was sweating.

Rosenblatt sighed, "I raised sons and was deceived."

"Why do you generalize?" I promptly came to the defense of the oldest son.

"Maya, you're right. I apologize, Eric."

The tension made me laugh and they both looked at me, confused. I got up, apologized for my cheerfulness which had been out of place, and left the office.

Chapter 22

Elena was ecstatic. She hadn't heard the voices raised in argument and she interpreted the vestiges of my laughter as a sign of my elated mood. The intimacy that had begun to form between us when she made up my face had started to take root and I prepared coffee for the two of us.

Elena spoke enthusiastically about the inspectors and their thorough scrutiny. I nodded and asked her how she was managing without her parents. "Don't you miss them?"

"What? Where is this coming from all of a sudden?"

"Your parents stayed back in Russia, right?"

"In Ukraine," she corrected and went to the sink to wash her cup. She came back and spoke quietly, in a low voice, saying that it had been difficult for her, at first, and that the longing had almost made her go her back to Kiev.

"And now?"

"What do you mean 'now?'"

"Don't you miss them?"

"I miss them, but I'm not a little girl anymore."

Elena was right, she was no longer a child, and neither was Daniel, though he was acting like a toddler who had tired of an old toy and wanted a new one, right away, no matter what. Moshe Levi wasn't a child anymore either, yet he was refusing to share his precious possession with the birth mother. I wasn't a child but, nonetheless, I was ready and willing to do everything to get back…

I realized that basically, that was my true goal: to bring the child back to us.

Moshe Levi neared the control room and I asked Elena to deal with him.

"I thought you two were friends," she said, but went to the window anyway.

The distraction I had enjoyed, thanks to the inspectors, was gone and, once again, I was overcome with restlessness. I re-read the article again, despite the fact that I could practically recite it by heart by now. Then I did something I had not allowed myself to do up till now, which was to search Google for the names Amos and Gila Grinfeld. There were several Grinfelds, but only one couple named Amos and Gila. I figured that requests for payment and bank statement were continuing to arrive at their address, and maybe they had a subscription for the weekly lottery, as if their fate was not common knowledge.

I glanced up at the grey sky which was streaked with yellowish vestiges of the sun's rays. Now I had their address; I committed it to memory and decided to leave the office half an hour early. Gil was picking up the children today, so I had time.

Without hesitating, I entered the address into the Waze app and was off.

Thirty minutes later, the recorded voice announced, "You have arrived at your destination." I stopped next to a private home with a gate that was flanked on both sides by a hedge.

I got out of the car and heard the sound of dribbling and a ball hitting metal. I came closer and peered over the trimmed bushes which were neck-high.

A small boy with curly, chestnut-colored hair caught a ball, let out an 'oof' and continued to dribble, once again trying to land the ball through the hoop. He missed. Once again, he cried out, 'oof.' That's the boy, something shouted inside of me, I know it's him!

Without thinking twice, I called out, "first stretch your arms, and only then throw it!"

Surprised, the boy turned around. "What?"

"You have to bend your elbows and then stretch and throw," I said, my heart pounding.

He just stood there, looking at me.

"You should, it will improve your shooting," I said, trying to convince him.

"My shooting is just fine!" he said, turned his back to me, and tried once more to score missing again. "Oof!"

"Listen, try bending your elbows first. It will help you make the basket," I continued, trying to encourage him.

"How do you know?"

"I coach basketball."

"You probably coach girls," he said disdainfully beginning to distance himself from me.

I panicked. Don't let him go into the house. I called to him, "Are you on a team?"

"No, I only play in the yard," he replied, again trying to make the basket and again failing.

"If you take one and a half steps closer and then release the ball, it will really help," I said, refusing to give up.

"I can't do it."

"Take one large step and then a small one, and then –

"I don't know how to do that," he cut me off.

"I can show you. Teach you."

He shrugged. "I'm not allowed to let strangers into the yard."

"Is there an adult in the house?"

"Of course. Shirly, my aunt."

"And your uncle? Her husband?" I continue to question the boy.

"She doesn't have a husband. She's not married."

Silence.

"Guess what kind of ball she is going to give me on my birthday?" he said, just as I was trying to think of how to keep the conversation going.

"A basketball!"

"No."

"A soccer ball?" I said, trying again.

"I knew you wouldn't be able to guess," he said animatedly.

"A volleyball? A handball? A tennis ball?" I said, trying my luck, but the best luck of all wouldn't be guessing correctly, it would be to getting him to keep talking to me.

"A hot air balloon!" he announced, with a tinge of victory in his voice. "She is going to take me up in a hot air balloon!"

I hadn't considered that. I expressed my surprise and admitted that I had never gone up in a hot air balloon.

"Shirly has. She says it's really cool," he stressed.

"What's your name?"

"Tom."

Tom was the name that we had almost given Dor. The trembling inside of me intensified.

"Do you really coach basketball?" he asked.

When I assured him that I really did, he glanced hesitantly towards the house and then approached the gate, opened it and gave me the ball. "So show me how to take a step and a half."

I put my bag down on the side, entered the yard behind him and showed him the step and a half. "One big step with your right foot, a small step with the left, and then – did you see how I made the basket? Now you try it," I suggested. He did what I had told him and threw the ball. The ball spun around the rim and flew out.

He was disappointed. I encouraged him to try again and, this time, he succeeded. The boy named Tom, who was real, not imagined, took a wide step and then a small one and sank the ball in the basket. His face lit up with joy. The coach in me noticed that his arms were relatively long for his body, a good quality in someone playing basketball.

My cellphone rang. I ignored it.

Then the door to the house opened and a young woman with streaked hair came out, dressed in clothes that seemed to be vintage or second-hand and wearing a lot of make-up. She lit a cigarette, noticed me and came closer.

"Who are you? What are you doing here?" she wanted to know.

Tom answered for me. "Shirly, this woman – " he looked at me and I said, "Maya."

Tom continued, "Maya, she coaches basketball! For Maccabi."

Shirly put her arm around Tom's shoulders protectively and lit into me. "And that gives you the right to be here?"

I apologized for coming in like that… "I was just passing by and saw him playing, then…"

Shirly became angry. "Let's see if I understand – you pass yards looking for children who play basketball?"

Tom ducked out from under her embrace and defended me. "I asked her to show me a step and a half."

"You know that you're not supposed to let strangers into the yard," she scolded the boy.

"But she's not a stranger! She coaches basketball. Don't you see?"

I hurried to apologize, admitting that I had been out of line, that I had gotten carried away. My phone rang again and, I ignored it once again, apologizing to Shirly once more that I had entered the yard without permission. I knew that I had to leave and get away, but Tom said that he wanted me to continue teaching him basketball, and so I continued to stand there.

Shirly told the boy to go into the house, but he refused. "I want to train with Maccabi. That way, I'll have something to do when you are out with your friends or resting in the afternoon."

"You have something to do – go do your homework!"

I couldn't help myself and intervened. "Don't worry, in our club, only children who do their homework and study for tests are allowed to train."

"Mommy would have let me…" the words burst out of him.

Shirly looked as if he had slapped her.

I apologized once again, took out the little notebook I always carried in my purse, wrote down my name and telephone number, tore the page out and handed it to her. "Here's my number. Only if you want it, of course."

Tom came to me, grabbed the piece of paper out of my hand and ran into the house.

Shirly turned her anger on me and said, "the show's over. You can go now."

"He's talented and he really wants to learn to play," I said, as I was retreating.

Shirly didn't react. She waited to lock the gate behind me then turned around and went back into the house.

I found it hard to leave and stood there for a few more minutes, hoping the boy would come outside again. The ringing in my bag shook me out of my torpor. It was Gil. I didn't answer but got into the car and went home.

Chapter 23

Everyone was happy to see me when I opened the door. Even Gil. He was certain that my lateness was due to the Standards Institute inspection and had called me over and over again to find out how it had gone. For a moment I had to concentrate to understand what he was talking about. I wasn't in that space anymore. I was in a world that revolved around the boy. In a world where I knew what he looked like, what he sounded like and that his name was Tom. I refocused my attention on the children, who were jumping around me, told Gil that the inspection had gone well, and that the representatives of the Standards Institute had been pleased with my work. Then, before he could ask anything else, I told him that I had found the address of Amos and Gila Grinfeld.

He didn't understand who I was talking about. I reminded him of the scientists who had been killed in the car accident and added that their home was only a twenty-minute drive from ours.

Gil's face froze when he asked what I thought I was looking for there.

"I saw him. He is thin, just like Shai. Light-brown hair like the three of them. He is so much like ours and his stance is exactly like yours…"

"That's enough! I don't want to hear anymore!" he said, and pulled away from me. At Dor's instigation, the children, who felt that they were being left to their own devices, became a train. Dor took on the role of the engine and began to pull his two train cars through the house.

"How could you have had the nerve to go there?"

"And you'll never guess what he was doing. He was playing basketball! You get it? Scientist parents and he plays basketball! If that's not a sign from heaven…"

"You've lost your mind. You will get yourself into so much trouble."

The train came in our direction, passed us, and continued on.

"His name is Tom. Just imagine…"

"I don't want to imagine anything."

"I wanted to take a picture of him, but – "

"It's a good thing you didn't. As it is, I know too much about him."

"I want to know everything about him."

Gil paled with horror. "Get a hold of yourself, Maya, before it's too late," he implored me.

"It's too late. Anyway, we can't continue living as if nothing happened."

"We can, because nothing has happened. We will continue to live as we have until now," he said emphatically.

His words seemed wrong to me and I stressed that, up till now, the boy's existence had only been theoretical. It's true that I had thought about him every day, however, that was imaginary. But now…

He stood before me indignant and I gathered up my courage. "Gil, let's file a claim in family court. No judge would deny us."

Gil sighed heavily. "Maya, listen to me. For the moment, I am setting aside what I feel and think and am telling you, in the most objective way possible, do not get involved in this. I'm not saying this as your husband or as the biological father of the baby that you gave up for adoption, but as someone who is looking at this from the outside." He spoke to me as if I was a client.

That made me angry. "Don't sit on the sidelines. Side with me on this matter. Come with me tomorrow, to the house, to meet him."

"No!" he said, cutting me off.

"We're going to Jerusalem!" called out the engine and the passenger cars behind him did the same.

"Why not?" I wanted to know. "Because of the law? Because this is a bit unusual?"

"Because he has a family and that is not us!"

"You're willing to give up on him, just like that?"

"I gave up on him a long time ago. You have got to let go of the past."

"Please help me," I implored. "What are the chances that we can get him back, if this reaches the court?"

I felt him making an effort to be patient, not to burst out. "If, theoretically, a judge listens to this claim, and if, theoretically, he is the child that we gave up, a lot depends on him. Do you understand that? The judge would want to hear what he wants. With whom he would want to grow up. The main consideration in these cases is the well-being of the child."

I became scared. "You mean, all of the adults will stand on the side and the judge will listen to Tom? He will ask him where he wants to live? With whom he wants to live?"

Gil said no, this wouldn't happen. "Do you realize that you are clinging to a boy who has no connection to you and that you are going to complicate his life?"

The train was coming our way again and the engine insisted that we join the train, asking to switch responsibilities. "Daddy, you will be the engine. Mommy, you're the first car," he commanded.

"*I am wast, de happy caw,*" crowed Ya'ara.

The train started moving. I put my hand on Gil's hips and felt Dor's hands hugging mine as we chugged from room to room.

A few hours later, when the children were finally asleep in their beds, I went to the living room and found Gil dozing in front of the TV. I wanted to caress his hair, which needed a haircut badly. I used to have to remind him to get a haircut but, ever since he had begun practicing law, he made sure to get regular haircuts. And now…

I shut off the singer who was singing a song in English as part of a competition to see who would represent Israel in the Eurovision contest.

The sudden silence woke him. For a moment, he stared at me with a vague look in his eyes then sat up straight and, as if life was back to normal, asked me if I remembered that next week was Purim.

Of course I remembered. My mother – as part of the change she had undergone from an active academician to a lively and energetic grandmother – had sewn the children the costumes they had asked for. When I was a little girl, she had spent long hours in the university's laboratories and would buy me off-the-shelf costumes; now she was indulging her grandchildren and sewing them costumes.

Chapter 24

The next morning I took an active part in getting the family ready for the kindergartens and work, trying to smile at Gil and act naturally. In an effort to push down the storm that was raging inside of me, I entered the plant, stamped my card and, as I approached the quality control room, remembered that Elena had asked for a day off and that I would be alone. Moshe Levi arrived straightaway, as if he had been lying in wait for me. His cheeks sported a short stubble and his eyes were glazed over. In a sheepish voice, he told me about the confusion that the woman was sowing in his family.

"Now my son has two mothers and I feel as if I have two wives. She comes over every day, sits for hours, talks about her pathetic life and makes Rose feel sorry for her. My son is at a loss. His initial enthusiasm has worn off. His biological mother is simply another woman, not an angel who came down from heaven."

I stared at him in silence.

"You're not saying anything," he said, suddenly catching on. "I'm talking and you're quiet," he complained.

"What is there to say?"

In my own story, which I kept to myself, the thing I wanted most was to see the boy over and over, especially since I had met him now and knew his name.

"You could say something. Give me some advice."

He wanted advice from me. That was rich.

"I can't give you any."

"Why not?"

"Because… because I'm on her side!" I blurted out. "Many years ago, I gave a baby up for adoption and today I would do anything to see him."

He looked at me, shocked, and without another word took the springs I had inspected, turned his hunched-over back to me and walked back to his station with heavy steps.

Despite admonishing myself for just having revealed a secret to the enemy, I felt relieved. I would no longer have to listen to his harsh words about the bad mother who had come to disrupt his family's life.

The hours left until the end of the day passed as slow as molasses and seemed never to end. At exactly 4 p.m. I left, going out into an overcast and chilly afternoon. The two young lemon trees that had been planted at the entrance as a gesture to the inspectors of the Standards Institute sported clear water beads. My purse hit one of them and shook off its shiny drops. The fact that the other young tree still had its drops on it bothered me and so I hit that one too and watched as its beads of water hit the sidewalk.

I didn't drive home. Over the past two weeks, my mother had become used to my deviations from the routine and didn't ask questions when I told her that I would be returning home late again.

When I reached Tom's house, the yard was empty. The sun had begun to set in the west and its rays were turning the cloud trails to gold. It was a small neighborhood. My son had the luck of growing up in a home with a yard. In the summer, he probably ran around on the grass, intentionally getting wet from the sprinklers, or he might lay in a hammock; in the winter, maybe he looked for snails on the ground. My musings were cut short by the rattle of a car entering the driveway. Shirly and Tom exited the car. I restrained myself from calling out his name or running to him. They were quickly swallowed up into the house. I moved to a better spot to watch the house. Opposite me was a window with wooden shutters that were half closed and on the window sill one could see a pot without a plant and some colored bottles. After a while, half of a woman's body appeared, then the boy, who had turned on a faucet, turned his face towards the window – that is, towards me.

I choked up from emotions and tears filled my eyes. I wiped them away and managed to prevent any more from forming.

Tom turned toward the woman next to him, said something and smiled at her. The smile remained on his lips for another split second as he turned his face back to the window. I caught my breath. He was smiling at me, I thought stupidly. I could swear that was Gil's smile.

I couldn't breathe. I leaned on the fence, feeling weak. Tom's movements seemed familiar to me. I could see the resemblance between him and Dor.

"Are you looking for something, for someone, ma'am?" A man's voice behind me interrupted my musings.

A man and a woman, both in their sixties, were standing in front of me on the sidewalk.

"No, no... nothing." I felt that I had been caught red-handed.

I turned to continue walking, as if I wasn't interested in the house in front of which I had stopped, and heard their steps, which I hadn't heard before, and then the creaking sound of the gate opening and closing. I turned my head and saw them entering the house. The grandfather and the grandmother.

Loud barking startled me. A large and hairy dog was running towards me, followed by a boy who was scolding him and looking at me suspiciously. Everyone probably knows everyone else on this quiet street.

I retreated to my car and, as soon as I sat down behind the wheel, I could hear the muffled ringing sounds coming from my purse. I unzipped it and pulled out the phone. Gil wanted to know where I was and why I hadn't come home yet. When I didn't answer before, he had called the plant and they had told him that I had left about an hour ago.

I blessed the mobile phone. At this point, I could be anywhere I wanted, I could tell him that I was at the supermarket or the cosmetician, or… I debated between the various possibilities and chose to avoid the question. "I'll be home in half an hour."

Without looking toward the house again, lest it place a spell on me and I wouldn't be able to tear myself away, I turned the key to the ignition. All at once, the heavens opened up. There was a heavy downpour and I felt as if I was steering Noah's ark on wheels. The windshield wipers were too slow for the amount of rain pouring down. Traffic was crawling and drivers were trying to find their way as if they were blind, advancing hesitantly and then braking over and over again.

I got off the main road and made a sharp right, trying to outrun the rain, until I arrived at an intersection where a long line of cars waited at a red light. Young men with white knitted caps were going from driver to driver, trying to get them to open their window a crack so they could slide through a bumper sticker which said, 'The time has come for the Messiah.' Really? I wondered. The eyes of the young man leaning into my window expressed disappointment that other drivers' refusal had pushed him in my direction, but he still hoped that I might prove more agreeable and he would be able to get rid of at least one of those stickers.

I opened my window a crack and he passed a blue and white sticker through it, thanking me with a smile that stretched from ear to ear. The traffic light turned green and I was able to crawl forward. One more round of lights and I'd be on my way. Suddenly the clouds, which had been lurking for their chance, opened up over the intersection. The young man who had lured me into taking a sticker knocked on the window on the passenger's side, bringing his face close to the glass. He had raised his jacket to cover his head and water was streaming from the upraised collar onto the window. I stared at him blankly, which he took to be assent, and grasping the door handle which I hadn't locked, slipped in, completely wet, drenching everything. The two back doors opened as well and another three wet and dripping young men entered. The smell of wet sweaters and coats filled the car and their breath fogged up the windows.

"She's one of us," the young man sitting next to me said, and he smiled proudly at his friends.

"Great, good, may there be many more," they replied.

The rain came down even harder and was very noisy as it hit the roof of the car. A small, round green dot could be seen through the deluge that the wipers were struggling to move from side to side. I lifted my foot from the brakes and pressed the gas pedal.

They burst out into a religious tune, chanting enthusiastically until the sound of my mobile phone ringing interrupted their singing. I told Gil that I would be a bit late and he asked me to lower the volume of the radio. "Let's talk at home," I said.

"What are you listening to?"

"It's raining."

"Rain?"

I disconnected the call. I let them out after two more traffic lights and it was only after I had parked next to the house that I discovered a package of savior stickers that they had left in the car.

It was almost 8 p.m. when Gil opened the door for me. We just looked at each other without talking.

"Mommy! Mommy!" Ya'ara cried out, her voice breaking the silence, and Gil let me pass.

I hung my purse up and went to the children. The three of them were already lying in bed, covered up to their chin with the duvet. Why weren't they asleep at this hour?

"Hi, my darlings," I said quietly, and they didn't jump all over me because they knew that once Daddy had taken the trouble to wrap them up in the soft blankets and tucked the edges under their bodies, no one was allowed to move. They smiled and Dor and

Shai began talking at the same time, telling me that they had made pancakes with Grandma and that she had allowed them to ladle the batter into the frying pan.

"Mommy, come to me," said Ya'ara in a commanding voice. I lowered the protective guard alongside her bed and sat down.

"Mommy, sing me a good-night song," she said, asking for a lullaby.

I wiped all thoughts from my mind and sang the lullaby that I remembered from my childhood and which now was part of hers. I extended one of my hands to stroke her silky hair and my voice shook. Very slowly, her breathing became quieter and deeper and her lips, which were sucking on the pacifier, relaxed and it fell out.

I rose carefully and went to the corner formed by Dor and Shai's beds, which were placed perpendicularly, and sat down on the rug between them. I also sang to them and stroked their heads, until their breathing became slow and protracted.

Gil asked me where I had been and why I had not turned off the radio when he tried to talk to me.

"It wasn't the radio. I picked up hitchhikers."

"A singing group?"

"Not exactly." Then he saw the packet of stickers that I had placed on the shelf.

"What's that?"

"The time has come for the Messiah."

"Yes, I can see that, but how did they get here?"

I told him where I had gone after work.

"Again?"

"I couldn't help myself," I said quietly. He didn't react. "I don't understand how you can be so indifferent."

His pupils contracted, a sign that he was insulted, but it was too late to take it back.

I sat down at the kitchen table and lay my head on my folded arms.

He sat down beside me, lay his hand on my head, and said that maybe a professional could help me rid myself of this notion that had taken hold of me.

"An exorcist?"

"Don't be cynical."

He took my hands and caressed them soothingly. Afterwards, he put one of my hands on the table, put his hand over mine and looked at me.

With a slow and hesitant movement, I placed my other hand on his and he completed the tower with his free hand. I joined the game, pulling out the hand lying on the table and bringing it up to cover his top hand, and he, in turn, pulled out his lower hand, placed it on top, and so, with our hands, we climbed the air ladder, one rung after another. At that point, I pulled my hands away and burst into tears.

Chapter 25

Three days passed and I found myself living in a fog, on autopilot, doing what had to be done at home and at work, working hard at keeping everything bottled up inside. On Wednesday, I felt that I couldn't do that anymore and went into Eric's office.

"Is your wife a good psychologist?" I asked, without a preamble.

He was startled and said that she was.

"Maybe…"

He shot me a questioning look.

"Never mind, I was just asking," I said, taking back my words, and making an effort to send him an apologetic smile, I left his office before he could try to get it out of me. My brain felt as if it was going to explode at any moment from the pressure that was building up day after day.

What was I thinking, I rebuked myself. That I could pour my heart out to his wife? I remembered the compulsion I had had as a child to light matches. Once, I had lit a whole box in one shot – it had burst into flames in my hand and I was burned.

I called a therapist about whom Sharon had told me wonderful things. Orna Naveh, very admired by my friend, apparently picked up on the distress in my voice and asked if I could come to her that afternoon since a patient had cancelled and she happened to have an opening. I sat down in one of the two armchairs in the small waiting room, as tense as a spring. I had never been in therapy before, not even during the crisis I had experienced after I was discharged from the army.

I was on tenterhooks and all I wanted to do was to get up and run, but I felt that I was chained to that chair and would have to make a herculean effort to get out. It would require courage as well. I wondered why both concepts were necessary – did it take courage to make this kind of effort, or did I have to make a special effort to muster the vital courage? At any rate, if I fled now, that would constitute cowardice, right?

Orna Naveh – a well-groomed woman in her forties – stepped out of her office and greeted me with a smile. She invited me to come in. In spite of the overwhelming feeling that I would not be able to free myself from the armchair and that I was a reluctant patient, I rose easily and followed her.

"I don't want to start by delving into the past and looking for repressed emotions," I announced, as soon as I sat across from her in a chair as comfortable as the previous one.

"You don't have to. You can talk about anything you want," she said in a calm voice.

"I have a specific problem and that's why I came here." I squeezed ten years into a few terse sentences and concluded by saying, "my husband thinks that I need help."

"And what do you think?"

What did I think? Do I need help? Did 'help' mean that I was ready to give up Tom and that all I needed was someone to help me do that?

"I think that I'm confused."

Her silence encouraged me to continue.

"I don't want to give him up. He's mine… ours."

She continued to gaze at me in silence. A tried-and-true tactic to squeeze out a confession. This theory had been proven by what my silence had achieved with Moshe Levi.

"The adoptive parents aren't alive anymore."

"Have you thought about the possibility that this may harm the child?"

"How? He will get back the parents who gave birth to him."
"And how do you think he will react?"
"Happily, don't you think?"
She was quiet.
Her opinion was evident. The 'game' was fixed in advance.
"Nothing can convince me that it wouldn't be in his best interest to have a complete family," I said, defiantly.
"And you thought that I could do my magic and help you get that," she said, in a low voice.
"I know that my reaction is an emotional one, perhaps even childish," I said, defensively.
"And a natural one," she added, this time warmly. "I want to help you but there is no magic formula. One session will not be enough to change your viewpoint or that inner urge which is driving you."
We were silent for a while, facing each other, and then I rose, paid her and thanked her for fitting me in so quickly, but did not make another appointment.

On the way home, Ruth called me and said, angrily, that I had overstepped by going to Tom's house. "You invaded their privacy, you gave them your personal details – "
"How did you know?" I cut her off, "You're spying on me?"
"I heard from the social worker who visited them. His aunt told her about the mysterious basketball coach who had come by…"
"A social worker?" I asked.
"Yes, the one who is handling Shirly's application to adopt the boy…"
"What?" I cried out, "That weirdo wants to adopt him? I wouldn't let her to care for a cat!"
Speaking sharply, Ruth said that it was none of my business and had nothing to do with me.

"But," I said, very upset, "everything about Tom has to do with me."

Ruth sighed and softened her tone. "Sweetie, it doesn't matter what you feel or what you think – you must not go there again."

"Why did she apply to adopt him?" I asked, wanting to know.

"Because she's his aunt."

"But I'm his mother ... if Gil only understood what I feel, we could – "

"Thank God, at least he has some common sense!" she cut me off. "I hope you won't let your crazy ideas ruin your marriage or your family."

"Ruth, don't give him to that woman," I pleaded. "She's uptight, she was suspicious of me, she argued with him in my presence. She looked as if she had just woken up. I'd like to know what she does at night..."

"It's none of your business," she repeated. "There are people whose job it is to find out all those things."

I asked her what kind of life he would have if he lived alone with her, and why shouldn't he have a better life, with us. And she said, angrily, that I was not qualified to determine what would be a better life for him.

"Instead of adopting Tom, she should get married and have a baby of her own. She's young, what's her problem?" I shouted.

Chapter 26

On Shabbat, several days after we called a truce, days that entailed forcing myself to come home straight from work, we went on a family outing to the stream that flowed at the foot of Mount Tabor.

We parked the car near the start of the hiking trail and began walking. Cultivated fields, small reservoirs twinkling in the sun, a path along the water channel. Every once in a while, the tranquility was broken by the roar of dirt bikes or jeeps that forced us to move aside so they could pass.

A plethora of brilliant red anemones, as well as blue and white ones, rolled out their carpet for us on both sides of the trail.

The level path gradually became an incline and we started to climb, following the clearly marked signs. I was breathing heavily and had to stop and catch my breath; Dor and Shai ran until they tired, asking again and again when we would get to the summit; Ya'ara had fallen asleep in the backpack on Gil's back, indifferent to the view and the effort expended in climbing.

We were a happy family! For the first time in a long while, I felt relaxed. Also, the steep path began leveling out and I climbed with stronger steps, even giving in to Shai's pleas to carry him on my back. After a while, Shai ceded his place on my back to Dor, who hugged my neck and put his head on my shoulder. I turned my head back to kiss his forehead and all of a sudden it occurred to me that, lately, I had rejected the fact that he was our firstborn and had handed that title to a boy that he did not know.

In an instant, the excitement I had felt evaporated and his hands felt as if they were pressing on my throat to the point that I was finding it difficult to breathe. The clouds became hazy spots that tarnished the flawless blue sky, and the summit – which up to this moment had appeared to be so close – seemed unreachable.

I conquered the strong urge to turn around and roll down the slope.

Gil was striding in front of me, his back partially hidden by Ya'ara who had fallen asleep, her head lying peacefully between his shoulder blades.

He finally stopped.

I put Dor down, sank down to the ground, looked at the crisscross of green and brown spreading along the slopes, and decided not to give up on Tom.

Ever.

I threw Gil a look. His happy and relaxed demeanor shook my resolution. How could I fight for my first child all alone? What chance did I have, facing the establishment on my own? My determination faded like a cloud that had decided not to let the rain fall, and had allowed its water vapor to scatter to the winds.

We had promised my parents we'd come for dinner and, when we got there, we woke the children from their restless sleep in the car. My father made his chopped vegetable salad and my mother was preparing a mixture made from the yolks of hard-boiled eggs to fill the now empty egg-white halves.

When Gil went to the bathroom with the children to wash their hands, I almost opened my mouth to tell my parents about their eldest grandson, the one they had never heard about. Maybe they would give me their support? But, before I could muster the courage to do so, Gil returned with the kids and the opportunity was lost.

We returned home and acted as if nothing had changed, as if our routine had been disturbed for a short time, but all was well again.

Chapter 27

Two days later, Danny Katzir came to congratulate me on the fact that the plant had been accredited according to the strict standards. "This time, I'm inviting you for a meal," he announced, gleefully.

I was not really hungry, nor did I really feel like spending an hour in his company, but I accepted his invitation. Lately I had been indifferent to whatever was going on around me, who I was with, or whether I ate in the plant or in a restaurant. I ordered couscous and Danny remained loyal to David's juicy skewers of meat.

"In the end, someone else did the work for you and demanded standards," I said.

"What's the difference? In the end, the results are what's important, right?"

"Anyway, you could have demanded this quite some time ago," I made a point of insisting.

He didn't have a chance to reply because the waitress came and placed plates of steaming hot food in front of us.

"I have a great joke," he changed the subject as he attacked his plate. "Why did the boy draw on the window?"

"You already told me that one," I said and the pleasant feeling that I had begun to feel from eating the delicious food evaporated and anger rose up instead. "It's a bad joke."

"You're right, it's stupid to tell the same joke twice," he responded.

The bitterness faded somewhat and I was only left with a burning pain. Doing my best to hide it, I stabbed my fork deep into my plate of couscous and raised it to my mouth.

"Do you have any children?" I asked, suddenly aware that I knew nothing about him.

"Of course, five, with three women."

"Five?" I was surprised. "Are they all on the kibbutz?"

"No, not at all. The two older ones live with their mother, in Canada. She met someone and took them with her when she moved there eight years ago."

"So you don't see them?"

"Of course I do. They come visit me every year or so."

"Every year or so..."

"My second wife lives in Tel Aviv, so I see the girls about once a month; but I see my youngest daughter every day."

I was quiet. How can one live separate from one's four children, missing out on almost every aspect of their daily lives?

The question of how it was possible to fall in love, build a relationship and to have it dissolve, not once but twice, was relegated to second place.

I stared out through the restaurant window. Thick, grayish uniform clouds covered the sky and sent down gentle rain. The week's break in rain had come to an end.

"You're really sensitive on the subject of children, aren't you? Maybe you should change professions... become a kindergarten teacher instead of working in a factory," he said, surprising me. I didn't react. The possibility had never occurred to me.

"Do you think that I always worked in the kibbutz factory? Nope. Before that I worked in the cow shed and, before that, in the orchards."

"So you think I should change profession and become a kindergarten teacher?"

"You've already accomplished your main objective in the springs plant, haven't you? From now on, all that's left for you to do is to maintain the status quo."

"And what's wrong with that?"

"Nothing. Maybe I'm wrong."

But he had succeeded in confusing me. So I continued to be silent, even when the waitress came by to take away the plates and pour us coffee.

Sometimes a stranger can show you the way – I recalled hearing or reading that somewhere.

"I heard a good joke on the radio today," I said, breaking the silence. "Let's see if I can remember it. One day, in the open-air market, a tradesman happened to pass next to a synagogue, and he was asked to come and join the prayers. He didn't want to and tried to get out of it by saying that he was forbidden to do so. They asked him why, and he replied that it was a proven fact that when he does not pray in the market during the day, he manages to sell all his products. They asked him what happens when he does pray and he replied, 'I don't know, I've never tried it.'"

Danny laughed and I figured that I had contributed to his collection of jokes.

On my way out at the end of the day, I passed by Daniel's office. The door was open and I peeked inside. Rosenblatt's younger son was busy emptying his office, putting his belongings in a carton. I was fascinated by this scene, his preparations for departure. Daniel was holding a device made of a spring whose coils were pitched and which was intended to hold business cards, and he turned it over so that the 'Rosenblatt and Sons Springs' cards fell out, as if his leaving had rendered them totally useless because of one inconsequential and petty detail – that it no longer was Sons, but Son.

He threw them into the wastepaper basket from on high, as if they were flyers thrown out of a small plane. Then, as if regretting his gesture, he pulled one out and placed it in his wallet. He straightened up and our eyes met.

"Good luck," I said to him and walked in the direction of Eric's office to hand him an order from one of our clients.

Eric wasn't alone. His father was with him.

"Life doesn't always go the way one wants," I overheard Rosenblatt the father say.

"Are you just finding this out now?" said Eric, surprised.

"No, but your brother is."

Father and son turned to look at Daniel's office and found me standing in the doorway. I entered and handed the order to Eric.

When I came home from work, the house was silent. I hung up my purse and was surprised to see lit candles spread out in the living room. "What is this... am I in the right house?"

Gil approached me, his face shining. "The children are sleeping over at my parents' and we... you and I, have the evening all to ourselves. Good parents have to think about themselves too."

I hugged him. "You're wonderful... what a great idea... a hotel room at home."

"Exactly. I prepared onion soup, bought a good wine and have some orange-mint bittersweet chocolate... but first, we will have a bath with the natural oils that I bought in the Galilee some six months ago. Usually, it's the children who play around in the water and we..."

"We have to prepare dough," I said, cutting him off. "Dor has to bring a challah to kindergarten tomorrow."

"Not wine?"

"Did you forget the gender revolution that the new kindergarten teacher introduced? The girls bring the wine, and the boys make the challah." I went to the cupboard and took out a bag of flour.

Gil had a solution. "Let's prepare the dough, knead it, and while it rises, we will spend some time in the bathtub." I felt so safe and warm in his love.

I put the flour in the bowl, added water, eggs and oil. Gil put his hands in too and we kneaded the dough together. "Foreplay with dough – we've never done that before..." he said, with a sexy smile.

Instead of enjoying the moment and going along with him, I couldn't help myself and said that maybe the dough was perfect, but we were missing a child.

Gil removed his hands from the dough with a sharp movement. "I had planned a romantic evening," he said, coldly.

"I'm sorry, Gil. Any other evening I would have been the happiest person in the world."

He washed his hands quietly.

"We have to do something," I said.

"Hey, let's kidnap him. We'll hole up on the roof of the tallest building in the city and demand that they either give him to us or we'll jump."

"Your dark humor isn't helping."

"What can I do. I've run out of 'white' humor."

All of a sudden, the sound of the doorbell broke the stiff silence.

I went to open the door. Ruth was standing there. She noted the candles and stopped, embarrassed. "Oh, I'm so sorry, I came at a bad time. I'll come another time."

Gil called out, sarcastically, from behind me. "No, come in, come in. Don't be fooled by the romantic atmosphere you see here." He turned around and began putting out the candles, one after the other.

"Did you come to tell us something?" I said, hopefully.

"I came to see Gil."

"Me?" he asked.

"Yes, I need your help. I being taken to court by the Ministry of Social Welfare."

"No way," he continued, sarcastically. "Sue you?"

"I will be called in for questioning soon."

"It's that serious? You must have done something very bad."

I told him that in fact, she had done something very good.

"The truth is, Ruth, that I don't really feel much like helping you," he said, dryly.

"What do you want from her? I told you that it was my fault!"

"Maya, I think that the dough has risen. Maybe you should go to the kitchen?" he suggested.

I ignored him and said to Ruth that I knew that Tom was the boy that had been on the news.

"You see what your interfering with the adoption has done?" he berated Ruth. That was the first time he had seen her since I had confessed to him.

She didn't say a word. The distress that she had been feeling recently showed on her face. The spark that had characterized her green-brown eyes, so similar to mine and my mother's, was absent and her face seemed to sag, as if it had surrendered to gravity.

"How could you?" he asked.

"I… you have no idea what I was going through, what condition Maya was in."

I burst out at her. "If only you had understood, at the time, how much I didn't want to give him up."

"That wasn't only up to me. You also have parents…"

"But they were away on their sabbatical. They knew nothing about this!" I reminded her.

Ruth sighed and admitted that she had told my mother because she had felt that it was all too much for her.

"But we agreed that we wouldn't tell them! How could you have deceived me like that?" I shouted at her in my frustration.

"Just like you could deceive me," Gil remonstrated with me. "Now, maybe you'll understand how I felt at the time, and how I feel now. Completely hoodwinked, over and over again."

Ruth expressed her pain. "Do you have any idea what *I* went through at the time? How this pregnancy affected *me*? Our family was so small. You are an only daughter, I remained single; back then… at the time, I wanted to adopt him myself!" she confessed.

"Actually, I thought that you were going along with Maya because there was a lack of good babies up for adoption," Gil said.

"Are you crazy?" she cried out, and stood up. "I think it's time for me to go."

"I think that Maya is the one who will go," said Gil, turning to me. "Didn't you want to take a shower?"

I had no intention of leaving.

"I don't know what to do," said Ruth, dejected. "I feel as if everything is crashing down around me."

Gil was merciless in his reaction. "That's how it is with serial crimes. One card falls and they all come tumbling down."

Ruth defended herself and pointed out that the complaint against her was regarding a completely different matter.

"Ah, so you're branching out…" said Gil, with a touch of cynicism.

"You hold a lot of anger toward me," she pointed out, sadly.

"I want you to stop talking with her about him. This terrible, immoral habit of yours, letting her know, must stop. It's over."

Painfully, Ruth said that her whole life was her work and her family. "You and the children. I'm afraid of losing it all…"

I almost felt sorry for her, but hardened my heart.

"For twenty years, I have been completely occupied by my work. It's been my life, and now…"

Gil's demeanor toward her softened and he asked her to explain what it was that she has gotten herself involved in and he would try to see what he could do.

I left them and went to the kitchen.

When they had finished talking, Gil went to the bedroom and Ruth came to me. "Don't go to his house again and don't try to contact him in any way. I'm warning you…"

"After you lied to me, you no longer have the right to tell me what I can or can't do," I berated her. "Do not let this adoption go through. Say that Shirly is not suitable to be his mother… investigate her. Find a reason to disqualify her! Do something or I will expose you! I will say that for nine years, you have been reporting to me…"

"Do you really think that I let you know? I only told you what you wanted to hear."

"I don't believe you. I'm sure that you have been following up on him all these years."

Ruth sighed and told me that I could say whatever I want to whoever I want, it wouldn't make a difference to her anymore because, after the conversation with Gil, she had decided to accept the compromise offered by the Ministry of Social Affairs that, if she resigned of her own volition, they would not pursue the matter.

That scared me. "You can't resign! Give me Tom back first!"

"You think you should have him just because you've decided that he is the baby you gave up for adoption," she said firmly.

"I know he is."

Making an effort, she rose wearily, as if an invisible weight was holding her down. She approached me. She probably wanted to hug me in parting, as we usually did. After all, she had always been like a second mother to me. Not anymore. My beloved aunt had betrayed me. If, at the time, she had not told my mother that I was pregnant, she would not have felt that she had to pressure me, at first, into having an abortion and, afterwards, to give up the baby for adoption. It was her fault that I had forsaken my eldest son and handed him over to other parents.

For so many years, I had hidden the birth of my first son from my parents. Now that I had found out that they had known all along and hidden that fact from me, I felt even angrier. Not only had they manipulated matters behind the scenes, but they had also never spoken about this to me and had let me suffer from the guilt of not telling them. Didn't they understand that was the reason for my depression after the army? Or had they known, but had preferred to believe that it was for other, less embarrassing reasons?

Chapter 28

The next day I stayed late at work. Anyway, it was Gil's day to be with the children. Towards evening, I climbed the stairs with a heavy step and found my key in my purse. But as I was fumbling to put the key in the door, it opened wide and a tall dancer stood in the doorway, looking very much like Gil. He was wearing a burgundy-colored leotard that stretched over his chest and muscular arms, and there were pink strips of chiffon material around his neck and wrists. Mouth agape, I took in the ballerina skirt enfolding my husband's hips and waist in curly pink folds, lifted my eyes to his mouth adorned with hot-red lipstick and to his blushing cheeks, stopping at his eyes that were made up in black and green.

"Swan Lake," he said, briefly.

My eyes dropped to the tights that encased his hairy swan legs which, instead of sporting webbed feet or ballet slippers, ended in black sneakers.

He sidled by me and went out into the stairwell.

"Where are you going?" I asked quietly, almost whispering.

"To the Purim party," he murmured and headed down the stairs, the folds of chiffon dancing up and down on his behind. I watched him leave but he didn't turn his head.

Yotam, our babysitter, was sitting on the couch, watching TV. "You can go," I said. I paid him and told him to leave.

There was a ballerina costume lying on the bed, identical to the one Gil had been wearing, except that the chiffon was white. When my hand touched the crinkly material, I remembered our first Purim, mine and Gil's. For our 12th grade party, we had dressed up as dancers, performed a piece from Swan Lake and won first place. That was before everything between us had fallen apart.

My fingers absently caressed the white chiffon and my heart turned over with sadness and longing. I called Yotam but it went to 'call waiting.' Without another thought, I burst from the bedroom, left the apartment, sped down the stairs, ran into the street and caught up with Yotam, asking him to return.

I called a taxi to take me to the address where Gil's office was having its Purim party. I had forgotten all about the party. By the time the taxi arrived, I had managed to turn myself into an elegantly made-up ballerina.

Can-can girls greeted the guests with glasses of hot punch. Balloons, ribbons and lights shimmered in clouds of smoke. I stood on the side, a wall swan, swallowing a drink that warmed my throat with searing sweetness, watching the dancers and trying in vain to find the pink chiffon tutu and black sneakers. Maybe he had left with a perky dancer to find consolation in her arms and I was searching for him in vain.

A mustached Charlie Chaplin approached me and asked me to dance. I put my cup aside and followed him, beginning to move with the frenzy. Everyone was dancing with everyone, taking shots of tequila. I became tired and dizzy from the drinks and the music, and decided to leave the craziness. All of a sudden, I noticed a swan wearing black sneakers standing on the side, drink in hand, eyes fixed on the dancers.

"Why aren't you dancing?" I said in a trembling voice.

He turned his head. "Maya!"

I raised one leg like a stork, turned on the other leg as I had learned to do so many years ago in ballet class, and ended in a bow. Gil grabbed my arms, and gave me a long and deep kiss with his greasy, rouged lips.

He's mine, only mine, how could I have ever doubted it?

Slightly unsteady, we went out to the car after midnight with me patting his buttocks which were very well-defined in his tights. He slowed down and walked behind me. "It's true. You have a great butt," he said whimsically.

"This reminds me of a poem by a guy – can't remember his name – who wrote about backsides," he said and added that we were lucky that the poet had decided to write poetry, otherwise that poem would never have been written.

He then continued to illustrate his point with other examples. I loved it when he was like that, a bit drunk. I took the car keys from him and drove home.

Chapter 29

In the morning, I felt heavy and my head was spinning. On the floor lay a pile of tights and chiffon and the bed was still filled with the memory of last night's eruption of senses that had pushed thoughts of everything else aside. Gil smiled at me as he gathered up the costumes from the floor, and I did not dare shatter the pleasant atmosphere by telling him that I had no intention of giving up on Tom, because I did not want to raise that wall between us again. However, it seemed that there was no wall standing between us but rather it was surrounding us, and we were unable to break out or break away from each other.

The next day, Gil went to the army for two weeks' reserve duty. This is my chance, I thought, excitedly. Without his discerning eye following my every move, I would be able to go, unimpeded, to the street where Tom lives, approach his yard in an attempt to communicate with him, in the hopes that he would be outside playing with his basketball again.

So, after work, I set out. My mother was home with the children.

Now that I knew of her part in my having given up my first child for adoption and the fact that she had hidden it from me all these years, I had no compunctions about leaving her with the children for longer and longer periods. The fact that I was taking advantage of her free time no longer bothered me.

I didn't really have a plan of action, and I didn't know what I would do if Tom wasn't in the yard, but he was there. Throwing the ball. When he saw me, he proudly announced, "I've been practicing the step and a half. Come and see."

"Where is your aunt?" I hesitated at the gate, which he had opened for me.

"Sleeping. She worked late last night."

I went in. He walked in front of me. His right arm rose and dropped in a movement which was a bit more forceful than the left, but that was the end of any similarity between him and Gil. Maybe he was imitating his mother's or his father's walk, or maybe he had a walk that was unique to him.

We played beneath the basket until he tired and stopped to rest.

"Are you a good driver?" he asked, suddenly.

"Yes, I think I am."

"Have you ever had an accident?"

"No."

"My parents had an accident."

I shuddered and stared at him, helpless.

"They died." His voice trembled and tears rose in his eyes.

I wanted to hug him and comfort him but my arms and tongue froze.

"Now, they are in heaven. That's what my grandmother said."

"Do you miss them?" I asked, and immediately regretted the question.

He turned his face away and didn't answer. I put out a hand to touch his shoulder but pulled it back.

"Do you want to continue playing?" he asked.

"Sure, of course, come on."

Come on, my brave boy, let's play and forget the pain.

The next day, I went to his street once again. When I got out of the car, someone called my name. It was Tom, standing there on a skateboard, smiling.

"Tom, what are you doing here?" I asked, and tensed up.

"Skateboarding," he answered, weaving left and right with ease.

"That's really good. Are you alone?"

"No, my grandparents are sitting there," he answered, pointing to a nearby bench. "Do you want to say hello to them?" he asked.

"No, I have to go."

"You should, my grandfather knows how to tell funny stories," he coaxed me, and continued to glide back and forth in front of me on his skateboard.

"Maybe another time," I said, declining with a heavy heart.

"Are you hungry? My grandmother brought some of her cookies."

My head was spinning from his constant movements in front of me and the afternoon chill that was stabbing me inside.

A pale boy skateboarded in our direction and stopped next to Tom. "Come on, already," he urged him. "They'll grab the rink before us!"

Tom turned and the two of them rolled away from me. I looked at them from afar and thought of all the things that I did not know about my son. What did he like to eat? What side did he sleep on? Did he remember to brush his teeth before going to bed?

Tom skateboarded out of the rink and once again rolled towards me with supple and confident movements. "Do you know how to skateboard?" he asked, panting.

"No, only how to play basketball," I replied, and was quick to add that I had to go. He asked why and I told him that my children were waiting for me.

"How many children do you have?"

"Three. Two boys and a girl," I answered, my voice choking.

"My age?"

"No, the eldest is five years old."

"I don't have brothers or sisters. I'm adopted."

I didn't dare make another sound. My hand went out to brush his hair and giving in to a sudden impulse, I hugged him.

When I let go, his grandparents were standing next to us.

"This is Maya, she coaches basketball," he introduced me proudly.

I smiled, embarrassed, stammered a few words of apology and, without looking at Tom or his grandparents, quickly distanced myself from them and fled to the car.

Chapter 30

Moshe Levi ignored me and only spoke with Elena, who had stopped wondering why there had been such a change in my relations with the angry-faced operator. He looked like a plucked chicken now and the change in him was so striking that Rosenblatt suggested to him, in very precise words, that he should take more care of his appearance and shave before coming to work.

Moshe Levi looked at him with a scowl, mixed with indifference, which did not improve his appearance. His cheeks continued to sport a salt and pepper stubble which he only bothered to shave now and then.

I felt sorry for this tormented and suffering man, and decided to fabricate a pretext to talk to him.

He was sitting alone. Lately, he almost never took a lunch break but rather remained like a guard on duty next to his machine, as if he was afraid that someone was planning to share that with him too.

"I can see that you're angry with me," I said after examining a long spring that had come out of the machine.

"Why should I be angry?" he said in a defiant voice that had a familiar ring to it.

"There really isn't anything to be angry about, and that's why I don't understand why you are avoiding me."

"What do you mean, avoiding? Am I obligated to speak with you?"

I was quiet and began to regret ever having approached him. For over a year I had been working in the Rosenblatt and Sons Springs plant near the silent and sullen Moshe Levi without any incident.

"I was an idiot for speaking with you about my personal problems and I don't want to talk about it anymore," he said.

"I understand, but if you change your mind..."

Then, for just a moment, he raised his eyes to meet mine and the lost expression I saw shook me to the core.

The next day, I was standing next to the window inspecting very small springs. They kept slipping through my fingers, as if they were trying to hide some flaw from me. The employee who had brought them to me was waiting patiently while I tried to get a handle on them.

Suddenly I heard a scream coming from the work floor. I dropped the small spring that I had finally managed to place in the caliper, raised my eyes and saw Moshe Levi writhing and yelling with pain, his hand covering his left eye.

I burst out of the room and ran to him. The worker at the station next to his arrived there before me and shouted, "Call an ambulance!"

I could see blood trickling through Moshe Levi's fingers. My telephone was in the quality control room and I ran to it, but Elena got there first. She was already reporting with urgency that someone had been hurt in the eye, and she gave the plant's address.

From where I stood, I could see the injured Moshe Levi sitting on a chair, supported by his co-worker. Other workers were crowding the scene. Eric maneuvered through the mass of concerned onlookers and placed a bandage on Moshe Levi's eye. The bandage became soaked with blood right away and was immediately replaced with another one. I went to get our first-aid kit. Elena turned very pale and I thought she might faint at any moment. "Do you think that he will lose his eye?" she asked, fearfully.

"Let's pray that he won't," I replied and scrambled through the kit to remove the appropriate bandages.

I reached Eric and handed him one of the bandages. He removed the one that was soaked with blood and replaced it with a clean one.

Moshe Levi groaned with pain and I didn't dare look at him. Grateful for Eric's calming presence, I went out to the plant's entrance to wait for the paramedics.

The wailing of a siren got louder and an ambulance with flashing lights appeared. It came to a screeching stop and two men dressed in white jumped out and pulled out a gurney from the back.

The wheels rattled noisily on the cement floor in wild tempo, just like that of my pounding heart.

After his eye had been bandaged, the paramedics placed Moshe Levi on the gurney and wheeled him back towards where they had entered. The gurney's wheels stopped suddenly at the slightly elevated threshold; Moshe Levi's body was jolted and he opened his one good, terrified eye.

The paramedics swiftly overcame the obstacle and the gurney was lifted into the ambulance and its doors were closed. It took off with a blood-curdling wail.

Eric held my elbow and asked me to come with him to notify Moshe Levi's wife.

Chapter 31

Rose answered the door wearing loose sweat pants and a red sweater that accented her black eyes and clear skin. Her hair was pulled back and she wore no makeup. For a split second, I forgot the reason we had come and focused instead on her demeanor. For some reason, I was expecting an older woman, one who looked worn-out.

"May we come in?" asked Eric.

She looked at us, from one to the other, trying to understand what brought us here, to her. When she took notice of our serious expressions, she indicated with her hand, somewhat against her will, that we should come in. There was an aroma of meat and vegetables simmering with herbs.

In spite of myself, I looked around with curiosity, examining Moshe Levi's home. The apartment was solid, well-maintained and sparkling clean. In my mind, I could hear Rosenblatt enthusiastically quoting Proverbs 31:10, "A woman of valor who can find? For her price is far above rubies," and my heart sank and I felt compassion for this woman and for what we were about to tell her.

"We're from the Rosenblatt and Sons Springs plant," Eric explained and, without delay, told her about the accident.

"Was there blood?" she asked, and added, "he's afraid of blood. He sees a drop of blood and bolts!"

"If you'd like, we can take you to the hospital," Eric gently offered.

"Yes, yes, of course. Just let me change clothes."

"Take your time. We're not in any hurry," I tried to calm her but felt a bit foolish, as if the problem was our time and not her husband's eye.

Eric and I were left alone. "A pretty woman," he pointed out, also surprised by Rose's pleasant appearance. "Reality can be so different from what we imagine."

"You've never met her before? After all, her husband has worked with you for years."

"I just never had the opportunity."

"Because you've never organized a social event for the plant's employees and family members."

"You're right. I always felt that that was more suited to large companies."

"It's too bad that the Standards Institute doesn't require it," I said, trying to lighten the mood.

Before Eric had a chance to react, Rose came back into the living room dressed in pants, a cable knit sweater and a light jacket.

"How did he get hurt?" she asked, as Eric pulled out of the parking space. Neither of us could give her an answer. We explained that it had all happened so fast that we hadn't had a chance to find out.

"He can't stand pain," she mumbled and her eyes met mine in the mirror.

"Like most men," I tried to lighten the tense atmosphere.

"Yes, once, when Adam was four," she began, caught her breath, and in a panic, said that she had to call their son, who was spending the night with a friend. "How could I forget him?" she mumbled, taking out her mobile phone and speaking into it quietly.

When the three of us rushed into the Emergency Room, we were told that Moshe Levi had been taken to the operating room.

After a long, nerve-wracking wait of several hours, the surgeon finally came out through the automatic sliding door which shut behind him in a whisper that did not bode well. His grave face displayed a feeling of defeat. He asked about our relationship to the patient and then spoke directly to Rose. He told her that they had gone to great lengths to try and save her husband's eye. He fell silent and his eyes were fixed on hers, as if seeking comfort.

She sank into the chair and then sprang up straightaway to ask the doctor if her husband was in pain. "He has no tolerance for pain," she confessed to the surgeon in a tear-choked voice.

"Who does?" asked the angel dressed in green. "Don't worry, he was given strong pain medication."

"And now, he…?"

"Mom, what happened? I came as soon as I could," a tall and broad-shouldered youth cut her words off. He stood next to her, his green eyes looking from her to the doctor and back again.

She hugged him, looked at him with tear-filled eyes, and told him in short sentences about his father's injury.

"So he will never be able to see with his left eye?" The youth found this hard to swallow.

"He has no left eye. He lost it," she explained, clearly.

He turned to the surgeon. "Was there bleeding? Did it hurt? He can't stand pain or the sight of blood," he said, as if he were repeating the family mantra.

In the end, the surgeon returned to his own battlefront; hopefully, he would have better luck later in the day and save an injured patient or two.

We stayed behind the closed door, helpless and at a loss for how to comfort them.

I stole looks at Moshe Levi's son, who did not at all look like the boy that I had imagined when I had listened to his father's painful declarations. Adam towered over the three of us and there was no doubt that his father had to lift his chin to look him in the eye. Adam was not only a tall young man but handsome as well.

In vain, I tried to find some physical parallel between his features and those of his adoptive parents; after all, they say that people who live together for many years, even if not related by blood, begin to resemble each other. Adam's eyes were very green, like forest leaves, and there was something confusing in the fresh pallor of his face. His nose was slightly flattened and he had broad lips. His forehead was visible because of his military haircut; it looked as if he was already preparing for the next stage in his life, and his cheeks were covered by a layer of light down, like a cotton field blooming with a new crop. No, in no way did he resemble his parents, not to mention that his broad physique which was in complete contrast to his father's slender frame. Suddenly he became impatient and I thought that he might be thirsty or hungry as he had been in such a hurry to come to the hospital and may not have managed to eat or drink beforehand.

"Would someone like a cup of coffee or a sandwich? There are vending machines here," I offered.

Adam looked at me as if he was seeing me for the first time and was perplexed by my presence.

"Let's go to the cafeteria," suggested Eric. "We have at least half an hour before they will let us see him."

A few minutes later we were sitting around a small table – Eric and I sat across from Rose and her son – haltingly trying to find words to fill the void. Adam was completely indifferent to our efforts, his two thumbs texting away at an impressive rate on his phone.

Chapter 32

Moshe Levi's hospital stay lasted five days; I went to visit him every day after work, always finding Rose at his side, attentive to his every need. You could feel the love between them and there was no trace of the irritable reservations which he had exhibited about her when he had poured his heart out to me. He turned to her gently, calling her 'Rosie,' and stroked her hand. She looked at him with great concern and called him 'Moshik,' her magic words turning him 180 degrees from the irritable Moshe Levi we knew into the pleasant Moshik.

I gave him Elena's regards, explaining that she wanted to visit him but had a phobia about hospitals.

"As of tomorrow, she can come visit me at home," he said and a small smile appeared on his lips.

The smile looked strange on his face. Actually, it didn't. It was just that I had never seen him smile before and it had taken this tragic set of circumstances for him to smile at me for the first time, a smile that softened his features.

I was glad that he would soon be released. He'd be more comfortable recovering in his own home and, although I was curious and had many questions, I refrained from asking him what was next, such as: had they decided what kind of therapy he would have to have and would they be putting in a prosthetic eye?

That night, I stood in front of the mirror in our bedroom and tried tying a narrow band of cloth over my left eye,

"What are you doing?" Gil said, surprising me from behind, and I looked at his image with my right eye.

"Trying to see what it feels like to see with only one eye."

"I'm surprised by your devotion to this guy," he said. He had just returned home that morning from the first week of reserve duty and had asked me about my week. I told him that I had been visiting Moshe Levi at the hospital every day. However, what I didn't mention was that I had also gone to see Tom every afternoon, that Shirly was warming up to me and was even grateful for my presence, as she saw how much the boy enjoyed playing basketball with me.

Now, Gil tied the band over both of my eyes, turned me around to face him and kissed my lips, my cheeks, my neck. "What is it like with both eyes covered?" he murmured seductively.

"Stressful. It's not like simply closing my eyes, knowing I can open them again," I replied, finding it difficult to succumb to his touch.

Gil removed the band in one swoop and I opened my eyes. "One learns to appreciate the sense of sight, right?" He covered my eyelids with fluttering kisses, but I opened them at once, as if they were really in danger of becoming shut for good.

The next morning, as I was crossing the work floor on my way to the quality control room, I glanced at Moshe Levi's machine and found that it had not been shut down. Liam, a relatively young worker who, since last year, had been learning to operate machines, was standing there. The production station had come to life under the guidance of another operator after having been shut down for five days.

I changed direction and approached Liam with mixed feelings, understanding that the production of springs using this automatic machine could not be halted simply because no one knew when Moshe Levi would be returning to work. Still, I was a bit sad, as I identified with the injured employee and his family.

"Good morning. How are you getting on?" I asked.

"Okay. I'm just getting started. I'll come to the control room in a little while," he replied, apologetically.

I looked at him. His medium-build and slim body reminded me of Moshe Levi, but that was the beginning and the end of any similarities between them. Curly locks covered his head and half of his sea-blue eyes.

"Make sure the measurements are correct," I said, unnecessarily, and hurried to leave him before another superfluous comment slipped out.

Instead of heading towards the control room, I went straight to Eric's office. He was concentrating on the computer screen in front of him but immediately noticed my presence.

"I saw that Liam is working at Moshe Levi's station."

"Yes, he's replacing him."

"Are you sure that he can do it?" I followed up on this.

"Yes, he's talented and eager. You yourself said that there was a future for the young man here in the factory."

"But I didn't intend for that to be at Moshe Levi's expense."

"Me neither, but…"

"I hope that Liam understands that he is a temporary replacement," I persisted.

Eric raised an eyebrow and was silent. I knew that I had strayed beyond the bounds of my area of responsibility, and that he was the one who was authorized to make such a determination, not me.

During the day, Liam indeed proved his technical ability and skill and, to my chagrin, the springs he brought for inspection were perfect. Trying to be faithful to his sullen and sour predecessor, I resented the excellent quality of the product that the good-natured fellow brought to the window with a smile.

Elena, who asked about the patient every day, but was not bound to him by a tangle of complicated emotions, admired Liam's accomplishments and heaped compliments on him. I hastened to dampen her enthusiasm regarding the new operator and pointed out that we were going to go visit the veteran technician at the end of the workday.

Her face fell and I could tell that she would have preferred that I forget that she had promised to join me.

I ignored her reaction and, at 5 p.m., we knocked on the door of the Levi family's home.

Adam opened the door and the bag on his shoulder indicated that he was on his way out.

His father, who was sitting in an armchair in the living room, his injured eye covered with a large bandage, called out to him: "I just came home from the hospital today and you're leaving already?"

"But Dad, you're not alone. You have guests." The lad tried to use us as a solution to his problem.

"At least come and sleep at home tonight," the father backed down, willing to settle for the minimum.

"We'll see. Bye. See you."

"Call to let us know," Moshe Levi gave in, talking to the closing door.

He sighed and, with a gesture of his hand, invited us to sit on the couch.

Elena asked how he was.

His good eye still fixed on the door, he mumbled that he was alright, and asked what was going on in the plant.

We sat with him and tried to carry on a conversation with him, but his mind wandered and it was clear that his heart was with his son, who had hurried to leave even though Moshe Levi had objected.

Rose, who had been out shopping, returned loaded down with bags. She was glad to see that we were keeping her husband company. It was obvious that his mood was somewhat improved by her presence and a shadow of a smile appeared on his lips.

She offered us coffee and her home-made cookies and the atmosphere warmed up a bit. Elena became more relaxed than she had been when we first arrived and joined Rose in the kitchen. They quickly returned with loaded trays. The four of us sat and enjoyed the coffee and cookies, but it was the women who conversed. Moshe Levi was silent and stared at the door, as if he expected it to open at any moment and his son would walk in.

After dropping Elena off at the bus stop, where she could catch the bus that would take her home, I drove as I had every day, to the Grinfeld family house to spend time with Tom. Those two weeks that Gil was on reserve duty and I was arriving home late every day, my mother didn't complain at all. She was certain that it was because of the operator's injury and my visits to him, and I didn't set her straight. Once in a while, my father would join her and I was confident that they enjoyed spending their free time with their grandchildren.

Even if that wasn't the case, I didn't care. I still harbored resentment towards them for their part in my having given my son up for adoption. I still felt an uncontrollable desire to take my anger out on them, although I wouldn't define giving them the opportunity to spend more time with their three beloved grandchildren as vengeance.

The next day, when I arrived for my daily visit with Moshe Levi, the door was opened by a strange woman. She was taller and slimmer than me and her hair was dyed platinum blonde. Something in her face looked familiar. Where had I seen her before? No, no, I hadn't seen her; I had a good memory for faces. But still, those broad lips, those green eyes…

"Hello, I work with Moshe at the plant," I explained and, though I caught myself before I added his last name as I normally would, I thought to myself how funny it would have been if I had called him by his first and last name in his own home.

"Come in, please. He's in the shower," she said, in a pleasant voice.

Rose appeared in the hallway and greeted me happily. "Hi, Maya, I'm glad you came. Eric was just here." Then she added, "Please meet Sarah. Sarah – Maya."

We shook hands and I realized who she was: the biological mother! My God, Adam looks just like her! It's no wonder that Moshe Levi stopped making perfect springs and couldn't concentrate on his work. His son's green eyes looked out at him from this woman's face and constantly reminded him of his failure.

We sat down in the living room. Rose insisted on preparing hot drinks, even though I told her that just soda would be fine. She went to the kitchen, leaving us to make conversation on our own. I was careful not to mention Adam, though I couldn't look at her without seeing his image right in front of me. Instead, I joined her in idle chitchat where we were simply trying to get to know one another.

She was interested in what I did at the plant and was telling me about her work as a dental assistant when Rose returned and saved us from the trivial chatter.

Looking at the two women, I drank my coffee and bit down on a cookie that melted in my mouth.

"Her cookies are delicious, aren't they?" Sarah said enthusiastically. "I have never met anyone who can cook and bake like her."

Then you should be happy, your son has been well-fed all these years, I thought to myself with unexpected bitterness. What was happening to me? Whose side was I on, anyway? I should be identifying with this woman, this green-eyed woman, right?

The patient came in and sat down in his chair, his thinning hair still wet, his face clean-shaven, and dressed in a light blue sweatsuit, a white bandage covering his left eye.

'Moshe Levi and his two women,' I mused and tried to hide my smile.

He refused Rose's offer of coffee and she didn't insist. She fussed around him, making sure that he had everything he could possibly need, but it was clear that she was not willing to give up her connection to Sarah, in spite of his strong objections.

"Where is Adam?" he asked.

And there it was, out in the open, the name that connected the three of them.

"He went with friends to plan their trip to the Golan," replied his wife calmly.

I expected some sort of objection from him, but he remained silent.

"That's the way it is at that age, at 18. They want to take on the whole world," Sarah smiled sweetly, explaining teenagers to me. "Under no circumstances do they want advice from adults. You probably remember yourself at that age," she added.

I studied her as she ran her fingers through her bleached blonde hair, and I wondered how old she had been when she had given birth to Adam. Suddenly I felt that we were accomplices, if only in a small way.

"I understand him completely," said Rose, standing up for her son. "He will be going into the army in two months and, until then, he wants to enjoy his freedom."

The door opened and Adam entered, accompanied by two friends, all three of them hungry and heading straight to the kitchen. "Mom, is there any food left?" he called out. Rose got up and apologized as she went into the kitchen to feed the young men.

Tom's image popped into my mind's eye and a shudder ran through me. The thought that, if I cut myself off from him as Gil and Ruth expected – basically demanded – from me, I would be able to see him again only when he turned 18, when he would be focused on his friends and indifferent to the adults around him.

I felt the urge to get up and leave that minute, but Sarah beat me to it and rose to go, saying that she had to get ready as she was invited to a wedding that evening.

I was about to get up from the couch and leave with her when Moshe Levi said, "Eric was here before. He came and offered me an increased compensation package."

I sank back into the chair, both physically and mentally shocked by what I just heard. "Increased compensation? He wants to fire you? Are you sure that you understood him correctly?"

"Yes. I will receive a lot of money."

"He suggested that you agree to being fired?"

"That's right," he said patiently. His expression was not one of anger, nor did I detect any disappointment or cynicism in his voice.

"What did you tell him?"

"I asked for time to think about it," he replied quietly.

"I can't believe it!"

"Why not? How many years can a person stand beside the same machine and manufacture the same springs?"

I was silent.

"This will make it possible for me to do something else. A change in life."

What was he talking about? A change at his age? What in the world could he do? I scrutinized his expression to be sure that he wasn't pulling my leg, and realized that I would have been more surprised had he been joking than if he was, indeed, seriously considering the offer.

"Since I was injured in a work accident, I am entitled to take a professional retraining course without having to pay for it," he continued, speaking in a surprisingly calm voice.

I kept quiet. I found it difficult to believe that he would so easily resign from a position that he had attained by slowly moving up in the ranks over many long years of hard work.

There was an oppressive silence and I felt very uncomfortable, as if I was stuck in an elevator with a stranger and didn't know where to look.

"Your son, Adam, is a handsome boy."

"Yes, we're lucky. We received a healthy and beautiful boy."

"He seems happy."

A small smile flickered in Moshe Levi's eye, and then slid down to his lips. "Your son is also probably happy with his parents," he added quietly. That was the first time that he had referred to my indiscretion during that moment of emotional turmoil in the plant.

Adam entered the room and saved me from having to react. He sat down next to his father.

"If you want to go back to the plant, I'll help you in any way I can," I said.

"No, I intend to accept the offer," he answered straightaway.

"And what about the eye?" I found it hard to leave it alone.

"I'm scheduled for surgery in two weeks and they'll put in an artificial eye," he answered.

"Ask for a blue eye, that would be cool," Adam suggested, laughing.

"If I ask for anything, then it would be one like the color of your eyes," said his father.

They both smiled. I got up. It was time to leave. Moshe Levi didn't need me anymore. It looked as if he had come to terms with the presence of another mother in the family, and he would bind his son to him once again by getting a green eye. He wouldn't return to the plant and it seemed that he was doing that willingly. I said my goodbyes.

He surprised me, extending his hand to shake mine. "Thank you for everything," he said with unexpected warmth.

Chapter 33

On the last day of Gil's reserve duty, I went to Tom's house after work and played basketball with him until Shirly came out with a pitcher of orange juice and ordered us to take a break. "When I think of how you chased me out of the yard in the beginning…"

Tom swallowed half a glass and went back to shooting baskets. We watched him and I said that he was a wonderful boy.

Shirly agreed with me and told me how she had fallen in love with him the first time she laid eyes on him. "He was only two days old and his face was already perfectly formed."

I felt my insides twisting into a knot. Two days old…

When I asked her why she didn't have children of her own, she giggled and said that all she had ever wanted to do was have a good time and draw… And then, as if she felt the need to share her private life with me, said:

"I supported myself by bartending in the evenings. I never went to college," she continued. "I wasn't made for studying. My sister got all the brains and I had ADD so, she became a scientist and me, a 'bohemian artist'… that's how she'd describe me," Shirly ended, in a sad voice. Then, perking up, she immediately added that all that was over now – she was finished with the night life. She had found a normal job. From eight to four. A friend had connections and got her a job as a receptionist for a building contractor. Her life had been completely turned inside out but, for Tom, she was ready and willing to wake up at the crack of dawn and work a whole day in an office…

We sat quietly for a while until Shirly broke the silence. "I wish the adoption process would end already," she said.

I remained silent and she continued to share: "In a week, the senior social worker is going to make a home inspection."

"A home inspection? What does that mean?" I asked her.

"She will probably want to look over the house, inspect Tom's room, and possibly ask all sorts of questions…" she finished, sighing.

"Do you have anything to hide?"

"No, not anything specific, but you know how nightlife is… boys, drinking, grass…"

"Did you say anything about that to them?" I asked, a sliver of hope cropping up in my heart.

"No, why? Is she planning to recruit me for the Mossad?" She sounded annoyed. "Anyway, that's all in the past. From now on, I'm as square as they come."

Gil returned home and I wasn't really happy about it. I feared his reaction when he'd ask where I had been all these afternoons during his absence and that made me uneasy. I wouldn't be able to hide it from him. Maybe my mother had already told him that I had been working late the whole time he was away, or maybe the children had said something innocently, like how much fun they had had with Grandma and Grandpa. I was better off confessing and thought that I should do so quickly.

I was tense but behaved normally. The children clung to both of us, as if afraid that we would disappear again. Over and over again, they asked for a story, a lullaby but, in the end, they gave in to their fatigue and fell asleep, one after the other, so sweetly that it brought tears to my eyes.

We left their room quietly and Gil placed his hands around my waist, turned me around to face him and kissed me on the lips. "I missed you," he whispered, and I cringed. Had I missed him or had I enjoyed the freedom to do whatever I wanted, to go wherever I wanted – the freedom made possible by his absence, and did I want it to continue like that? My thoughts frightened me, and I responded to his passion. He led me to our bedroom, undressed me quickly, got out of his clothes and made love to me tenderly and eagerly.

For a while, we were only a man and a woman in a bedroom, without the responsibility of children, without any conflict that might threaten to tear us apart. I was almost tempted to fall asleep curled up in his arms and stay silent, but knew that it would be worse if I put it off, so I told him the truth. That did it. I had ruined the pleasant homecoming. He didn't respond. He didn't say a word. He only shifted away and turned his back to me. I didn't dare touch him or say anything. Not that night.

The next day, I picked up the children from their kindergartens and paid a lot of attention to them, with the slim hope that Gil would come home in a better mood and I would be able to fix what I had broken.

But he came home after the children were already in bed, went straight into the shower and then started dressing to go out. I was surprised and asked him where he was going.

"I am going to meet Hoffman in a restaurant in Herzliya."

"He's coming alone?"

"He's coming with his wife. Daria will join me."

"But I don't have practice this evening," I tried to say.

He didn't react.

"You didn't even ask if I was free to join you," I said, sadness overcoming me.

"You're busy with other things, aren't you?"

I didn't say anything.

"Have you stopped going there? Are you going to be rational and stop seeing him?"

Helpless, I stayed quiet. I couldn't make a promise that I couldn't keep.

"You understand why I didn't ask you to come with me?" he said, as he went to the door.

"One has nothing to do with the other," I protested.

"If his aunt knew that you are a Trojan horse… that you are fantasizing that he is your son…"

"I'm not imagining it! Soon I'll have proof. I took a straw that he used and sent it to a genetic laboratory," I burst out, and told him what I had been planning to hide, at least for the time being.

"So now we're a chapter in 'Sherlock?'"

"Let's see what you have to say when the results come in and his DNA proves that he is ours."

Gil glared at me and said that the children were feeling that something was off with me. "You are neglecting them and you've abandoned the girls on the team, the girls to whom you gave everything, invested your time, your effort, your soul. They lost the competition."

"That has nothing to do with it!" I retorted angrily.

"It has everything to do with it!"

"So you're angry with me and are running to Daria…"

Gil approached me and said that he was willing to call Hoffman and Daria right now and cancel the meeting in the restaurant, on condition that I stopped going there and put an end to it all.

I wanted to say yes, to get our pleasant life back, the sweet routine of parents with their three children, our good relationship where intimacy flowed so easily. But I couldn't say a thing. My throat choked up, and silence lay between us like a predator ready to pounce, until Gil shot it down. "Do you understand why I'm going with Daria?"

"You abandoned me then too."

"Don't be so dramatic. I'm not leaving you," he said, coldly.

"You got scared and you ran."

"That's enough, you're reacting as if what happened then is happening now," he said.

"Don't you understand that everything that happened then *is* happening now, again?"

"Yes. In your head, it is. Go to a psychologist! A shrink might be able to help you…" he said, vehemently.

"You go! You're the one with a problem. A father who doesn't want his own child!"

"My only problem is you!"

He couldn't have hurt me more if he had slapped me. Before he turned to go, I asked him if he regretted our meeting at the Maccabi field. "Because if we hadn't met again, maybe you would have had a better life."

"Until a week ago, my life with you was a very good one," he pointed out.

"Could be, but maybe you never forgave me for the fact that you were saddled with a family earlier than you had planned."

"The only thing I never forgave you for was that, without my knowledge, you turned me into a person who gave up his baby for adoption," he said, and left.

That night Gil returned late. I was awake, waiting for him, hoping that our duvet would bring us closer; but there was no hope of that happening because, just like a cliché in an old movie, he strode into our room with purpose, went to the closet, grabbed a pillow and blanket from the top shelf and went to go sleep on the couch in the living room.

Neither of us had ever done that before.

My head rang with another cliché – 'there's a first time for everything.'

I couldn't fall asleep and twisted restlessly in the bed, a bed that was too big for one woman, a woman filled with sadness. Before sleep finally gathered me up in its arms, I remembered how, during those two weeks that he had been on reserve duty, the option of sleeping diagonally had been, in fact, a very comfortable one.

Chapter 34

Around noon the next day, Eric met me on the work floor and asked if I wanted to go to the Asian restaurant again. I was surprised. He hadn't been sending me improper looks lately.

"We came out pretty well from Moshe Levi's accident," he said, explaining the reason for the invitation.

"Is that a reason to celebrate in a restaurant?"

"Celebrate? What are you talking about? I simply wanted to enjoy a meal and talk with you a bit together, away from the plant."

"Okay, let's go. We'll order the fish, one that will look up at us from the plate with one eye," I agreed.

"Cynicism doesn't suit you," he said.

Having lunch at the company's expense, when I found it difficult to concentrate on work anyway, suited me perfectly. All day, I kept visualizing Gil and Daria enjoying themselves in an expensive restaurant with Hoffman. Based on the late hour he had come home, maybe they had continued the merriment, only the two of them, who knows where…

Even now they were together at work. They were probably having a work-related conversation about legal files, but it could easily develop into one that would cover other topics, branching out like offshoots of a tree.

Maybe they were going out for lunch together, going to an Asian restaurant or to an expensive meat restaurant that was more to the younger attorney's taste. Maybe they were playing truth or dare, like during their previous dinner with Hoffman and his wife. Maybe Gil told her: One – My baby was given up for adoption when I was 19. Two – I married young because my wife freaked out. Which of these two sentences would Daria think was a lie?

Eric cut through the scenarios running through my mind and asked that, regardless of where my thoughts were, would I please cut them short and be with him in the here and now. I managed to follow his suggestion and enjoyed the meal, which was pleasant and tasty.

Towards the end of our meal, Eric said that I deserved a bonus for my success with the representatives of the Standards Institute. I was surprised. Several weeks had passed since that day and he was mentioning this just now?

"Not money. Fun. Bring a bathing suit tomorrow and be prepared for a surprise."

What was he planning? What does fun as a bonus mean?

Any other day I would have refused his proposal but after last night my conscience was less rigid.

That afternoon I returned home on time and Gil arrived just after me. We behaved with polite restraint and were perfect parents. That night, he once again chose to sleep on the couch, thereby erasing any hint of doubt I might have had regarding the fun that Eric had suggested.

In the middle of the night, I woke up in a panic. He was going to leave me. That's what was going to happen, perhaps sooner than later. I would lose Gil and who knows if I would win Tom. I decided to cancel the fun-day with Eric – I'd call in and say that I wasn't feeling well and couldn't come in to work. I would prepare Gil's favorite marble cake, tell my mother that there was no need for her to come in the afternoon, that I'd pick up the children myself… and forfeit my visit with Tom.

This plan calmed me, but I was still unable to fall back asleep. Instead, I tossed and turned in the large, empty bed until I fell into a restless, dream-filled sleep. However, I couldn't remember the dreams when I woke up in the morning.

Despite my efforts to be cheerful and melt the icy wall that was currently under construction between us, Gil was cold and distant. I told myself that this would justify me relinquishing the plans I had made during the night while in the throes of my fear. I threw my one-piece swimsuit, the one I had bought the previous year and had barely worn, into my bag and rushed out the door.

Eric's car and mine were parked one behind the other, then only mine remained in the lot and Eric's was floating along the wet highway. In the front seat sat a man and a woman who were trying very hard to carry on a flowing conversation, until the threads of the conversation gradually broke off and a comfortable silence took over – a silence that wasn't awkward the way it might have been between two strangers, but neither was it the relaxed, unspoken intimacy between friends or lovers.

The car barreled northward, then east, and began ascending Mount Carmel.

"Where are we going?" I asked.

"So you're finally curious. We're going to the spa hotel in the forest," he announced, enthusiastically.

I was immediately on the alert and felt my cheeks blush.

"A hotel? I thought you said something about swimming."

Eric laughed. "What are you so nervous about? I didn't reserve a room for us! There is a great health club there, at the Carmel Forest Spa Resort. It's quite exclusive. You've probably heard of it. I thought that it would be an enjoyable and pleasant change to swim there and perhaps have a treatment."

I was embarrassed and my cheeks became very warm.

It was raining on the mountain; raindrops were landing on the pine needles and then dropping to the ground. On the other hand, the indoor pool was warm and inviting. The chlorinated water ran down my exposed shoulders each time my upper body emerged from the depths and I came up for breath.

Eric stood on the edge of the pool preparing for his next dive. He had an athletic body without an ounce of excess fat. He looked at me and smiled, then made a perfect arc into the water, disappearing underneath and rising again like a dolphin.

I thought of Gil who could not be convinced to swim, not in a pool nor in the sea. "I wasn't born with gills nor a tail," he would joke while adamantly refusing.

I turned to float on my back, and then rolled over again and dove to the bottom to divert my eyes from the sight of Eric's body. When I came up again, he was floating close to me, trapped me with his arms, pulled me under the water and attached his lips to mine.

For a split second, I responded to the wet kiss, then quickly wriggled out of his arms and hurried to the surface to fill my lungs with oxygen.

An hour later, we entered the Turkish bath, a round and spacious room filled with white steam. Two men were sitting catty-corner from us at the other end, exchanging views on women's breasts.

Eric and I had wrapped our towels around us.

One of the men said, "I don't remember where I once read an article that said that all men think about breasts, even revered university professors. It suggested that academic titles be given to breasts – not to those who think about them – and should be allocated according to size. For example, smaller ones would be teachers' assistants, mid-sized ones Ph.D. candidates, and the large ones, tenured professors."

Eric smiled and I found myself thinking about what academic title would be appropriate for my own pair. When we left the steam room to breathe some fresh, cool air, I thought that our day at the spa had come to an end, but it turned out that he had ordered massages for us and, for an entire hour, I handed my aching muscles and anxious mind over to the wonderful hands of a masseuse. She skillfully found all of the vulnerable and tense points in my body, kneading and loosening them until I simply melted away, as did all of the negative thoughts lurking around, threatening the euphoric experience.

If I thought this day of pampering was over, Eric hurried to point out my mistake and announced that now it was time to eat and that the meals here were exceptional.

We entered the dining room whose tall windows overlooked the trees of the Carmel mountains, and the hunger which I had suppressed until now suddenly came to life at the sight of the colorful buffet laden with goodies.

"Everything they serve here is very delicious and based upon a healthy diet of fish, vegetables, whole-grain breads," said Eric, heaping praise on the top-notch cuisine. "I come here often and have never been disappointed."

I wondered who else he'd brought here; how many others had earned a fun bonus like this?

I chose peppers stuffed with burghul and lentils in a spicy tomato and herb sauce, a mushroom burger served with scalloped roasted potatoes, and a spinach salad with orange slices – dishes I had never tasted before. Everything was absolutely delicious.

On the way back south, we were satiated and exhausted and just enjoyed the music on the radio. My body, which had been subjected to unexpected pleasures all day, relaxed in the seat and my eyes were almost shut. When the car stopped, I thanked him for the bonus and said goodbye.

Behind the wheel in my own car, reality began to set in, crushing the pleasure I had just experienced, banishing the sweetness of the day, and inviting bitter thoughts to take over. What kind of 'bonus' would Gil give Daria should she bring a legal victory to the office?

Chapter 35

At the house, the cold war was still on. It took all my determination to refrain from going to Tom's house but, two days later, Shirly called me and asked if I could pick up Tom from basketball practice in Maccabi. It was her first day at her new job and she hadn't planned her day right. I debated about how to respond but, just then, Gil sent me a message saying that he had to stay at the office until evening, and so I jumped at the opportunity to help her out and sent her my address.

Tom and I came home drenched. "What a rainstorm. Who would have thought that there would be so much rain in April? I already took my umbrella out of the car," I said. "You're completely wet. I'll look for something for you to wear. Go take a shower, there's plenty of hot water."

But Tom didn't want to take a shower. He was still upset. "I don't understand why Shirly didn't come to pick me up today."

"I told you. Because of her new job."

"So why doesn't she answer her cellphone? I want to talk to her."

I tried to calm him down. "Everything's OK. I left her a message and she'll probably call as soon as she has a chance."

But Tom wanted to go home. I brought him clothes that would fit him. A neighbor with a nine-year-old son had brought me a bag of 'hand-me-downs' in good shape. "It was a shame to put them in the recycle bin. They'll be better off in your closet, waiting until Dor can wear them.' And now, less than a month later, I was able to put them to good use.

"Here's the bathroom. Leave the wet clothes on the floor and I'll put them in the dryer. Shall I make you some hot chocolate?"

He turned towards the bathroom reluctantly and didn't answer.

"I make great hot chocolate from real cocoa powder."

He wasn't impressed, and went to change his clothes.

A few minutes later, he returned wearing a dry sweatsuit, still upset that Shirly had not come to pick him up after practice.

"She probably got held up at work," I said.

I gave him the hot chocolate; he took one sip and put the cup down. "My mother was never late and never stayed late at work. What if Shirly doesn't know how to be a mother?"

I didn't get a chance to answer when he kept asking where my children were.

"With my parents," I began to say, when suddenly there was a deafening thunderclap, as if it was trying to roll into the house.

"Don't be scared, it's only thunder," I said quickly, controlling my urge to hug him. I was afraid that he would resent it.

"I'm not scared."

"You know what, let's do something fun until Shirly gets here. We have lots of children's games, though they're for younger children, but maybe you'll find…"

"I don't have any brothers or sisters."

"Me neither."

"You're adopted too?"

I smiled and said that I wasn't. I so wanted to tell him about my parents, the scientists, who had said that I was enough for them because they were so busy with their research, studies, lectures, and traveling abroad, but Tom cut me off and told me that he has four cousins who live on a moshav, and they have a dairy farm and a huge avocado orchard, like a forest. He ended with, "This Saturday, I'm going there with my grandparents."

Once again, we sat in uncomfortable silence.

Tom noticed the chessboard, went to it, and poked the pieces with his finger. "What a nice chess set. Can I play with the white knight?"

"Sure, of course."

He picked up the knight carefully and felt it. "The black knight too?"

"Sure, of course – with all the pieces."

The door suddenly opened. I was alarmed. Who could it be? Surely not Gil. His meeting was supposed to last until at least 8 p.m. But there he was. I was in shock. What should I do? "Hey … didn't you say that you would be coming home late?"

He took off his coat, hung it up, and explained that there had been problems with the electricity in the office and so they had put the meeting off till the next day. Then he noticed Tom.

There was no way out of it; the truth would come out. "This is Tom," I said straight away. "His aunt couldn't pick him up after practice and asked if he could wait here. Tom, this is Gil, my husband," I managed to get through the introduction.

Gil didn't move, darts shooting out of his eyes.

"Nice to meet you," said Tom politely.

Gil just stared at him for a moment and Tom continued, apologetically, "Maya let me play with the knights."

Gil turned his attention back to me and hissed at me. "You've crossed the line! How dare you…"

"Are you angry because of me?" asked Tom fearfully.

I didn't wait for Gil's answer and told Gil that there was pasta and chicken patties and that I could warm them up for him.

"I'm not hungry," he said, coldly.

"Do your children play chess?" asked Tom, and I replied that they didn't, that they were still too small.

"My father taught me to play chess when I was five."

Gil looked at him for a moment, dumbfounded, then looked away. "Well, I'll be going."

"Are you angry that I took your knights?"

"No, no. What are you talking about?" my husband answered, in spite of himself.

"Can I play chess with you?" The child did not give up. "Please, just until Shirly gets here."

Gil didn't know what to say.

"I always play with the white," said Tom.

In a very quiet voice, Gil said that he didn't mind either way.

Tom went to the chessboard, replaced the black knight and sat down in front of the white pieces. Then he took a carved white knight out of his pocket and stroked it. "Can I use this knight? My father carved it for me because the one in our set got lost. I always carry it in my pocket because I'm afraid to lose it."

Gil gave in. "Sure, of course." He threw me a blazing look and went to sit in front of the black pieces, as if he was being held hostage.

Tom said that he would start, moved a pawn, leaned back and looked at Gil expectantly.

After what seemed like too long a pause to decide on an opening move, he said to Gil. "It's your turn."

I took his wet clothes to the bathroom to put them into the dryer and returned to the battlefield, but did not approach. Instead, I followed the scene from afar.

After a few moves, Gil told Tom that he was a good player.

"My father said that I was natural."

Gil raised his eyes and let them linger on Tom's demeanor. My heart constricted.

"My father, he was an astronomist… he might have discovered a planet that no one has ever seen. He showed it to me in a special telescope. We were thinking about what to call it."

"Your turn," said Gil, perhaps contemplating Tom's words.

Tom came back to the present, glanced at the board and moved the carved knight. "He always played with me for real. You're not letting me win, are you?"

"No, of course not. Here you are. Check."

"Oops, why didn't I see that?" said Tom, disappointed in himself. "You can get out of it."

Tom studied the board, then raised his eyes to Gil. "Don't tell me."

"Of course not. We're playing for real, right?"

"I haven't played in a long time, not since my father…" He concentrated on the board. "I found it!" He moved one of the pieces and threw Gil a victorious look. "Is this what you meant?"

"No," said Gil, and stared at Tom for a long time.

"I got you!"

"You have no idea how much." He looked at the board again. He moved the bishop and announced, "check."

"Again? I thought that…"

"Always think several moves ahead," Gil said to him quietly. "When you move one piece, it affects the whole board."

"I know that."

Gil continued talking as if thinking to himself. "Life is like that too. You make a move and that affects everything around you."

"Like the camel that went on the road and hit my parents' car. My grandmother warned them that donkeys cross the road and, in the end, it was a camel."

Gil looked at him and said in a sad voice, "sometimes, things happen and we have no control over them."

"I almost went to Eilat with them but, in the end, I stayed home with Shirly. She said that it was heaven-sent and my grandmother said that there is a God in heaven. That's the same thing, isn't it?"

Gil looked at him and nodded.

"Shirly will adopt me… did you know that this is the second time that I'm being adopted?"

I could see that Gil was unsure of how to react but I did not dare intervene.

Tom continued to quote his grandmother. "My grandmother says that God loves me because he saved me from the camel and gave me Shirly, and that I should be glad about that."

In a strangled voice, Gil said that she was right. She was very smart, his grandmother.

Tom concentrated on the board, planning his next move, and moved his rook.

The doorbell rang.

I went to the door. Shirly was standing there, her hair cut in a nice carré and wearing an attractive tailored pantsuit. I stared at her in amazement, trying to reconcile her appearance with that of the unkempt young woman, the only Shirly I had ever encountered.

She apologized for being late. "It's because of my new job. At 3:30 p.m. they called everyone in for an unscheduled meeting and I couldn't get away… I can't afford to lose this job … next time I'll line up a babysitter just in case. Soon we'll be living near my parents; then everything will be simpler…"

I reassured her and said that it was fine, there was no need to apologize.

"I'm truly sorry. Please don't tell anyone about this," she added, stressed.

"Who would I tell?" I asked.

"I don't know. Anyone. I don't want to think what might happen if anyone found out just now… as it is, I'm terribly nervous… I'm under great scrutiny and I have to make a good impression."

We strode over to the chess players. Gil took the white king down with his black bishop and announced, "checkmate."

"Oof. You beat me," Tom said, disappointed.

On the inside I was shaking, but outwardly, I was trying to act like everything was normal and introduced Shirly to Gil.

Gil nodded without extending his hand. Shirly acknowledged him with a short movement of her head and turned to her nephew.

"Tomush, I'm sorry I was late."

But Tom's attention, which before had been very troubled, was directed only at Gil, who was rapidly returning the pieces to their rightful positions. "Can we play just one more?" Tom asked.

"I'm sorry, I have to go back to the office," said Gil and handed him the hand-carved white knight.

"You play so well, you might have even beaten my father." Gil froze. Then he placed the last pawn in the last empty space.

Shirly hurried Tom along, reminding him that he still had to study for a test, thanked me once again, and the two of them left.

Chapter 36

"You crossed the line," said Gil, raising his voice, and then, the anger that had been boiling up inside for the past half hour exploded and he slammed his hand into the chessboard and the pieces abruptly became airborne. I knew that no apology or plea for forgiveness would help. Although it had not been my intention, I had, in fact, forced him to meet Tom.

"I'm going to pick up the children. Best you not be here when I return," he said to me in a harsh voice.

"What? What do you mean – not be here?"

"It's very simple. Don't be here," he repeated the command, his voice icy.

"You are kicking me out of the house?" I was stunned.

"That's exactly right," he replied and turned towards the door.

I grabbed his hand. "Gil, stop talking like that. You don't mean it."

He wasn't leaving me or our home because of what I had done in the past, that nagging fear I always had, but was telling me to go because of what I had done now.

He shook off my hand and, in a cold voice, said that he no longer recognized me, that I had become a stranger, and opened the door.

"Gil, I love you, I didn't do it on purpose – you weren't supposed to be home yet, so ..." I begged, but he ignored me and left, slamming the door behind him. I stared at it as if he had locked me inside the apartment. I sank to the floor in despair, wishing the tears to pour out so that I could let go of the tension, the anxiety and the fear; the soft tears that were running down my cheeks were unable to ease my pain.

I didn't want to go anywhere. Not to my parents and definitely not to Ruth. I went into the bathroom to wash my face. Tom's clothes were still spinning around in the dryer. I stopped the machine and took them out. I buried my face into their warmth and suddenly knew where I would go; the best place I could go to if I was, in fact, exiled by Gil.

A half hour later, Shirly opened the door. "Oh, you didn't have to come especially for that. He has enough clothes in his closet," she said, as I handed her the folded clothing. "Such a bother for a few pieces of clothing, I feel indebted to you as it is …"

"It's fine. Where's Tom?"

"He's sleeping," she told me the obvious – it was already 9 p.m. "Your children are probably asleep too."

I nodded and remained standing in the doorway. "Would you like to come in? Drink something?"

I agreed right away and came in before she could rescind her invitation. "With pleasure… coffee… instant, no sugar," I said as I followed her to the kitchen. "Tom didn't stop talking about your husband," she said. "He's probably a good father."

She noticed that I wasn't speaking and asked if I was okay.

"I'm fine. Could I go look in on Tom for a moment? I've never seen him asleep," I said.

She gestured with her hand, a kind of consent, but her face expressed how odd she thought the request was. For a moment it seemed that she might follow me, but she stayed in the kitchen and let me go be with my son.

When I returned to the living room, I sat down on the couch and did not show any signs of leaving, mainly because I had no such intentions. I had decided to stay and sleep there, despite the fact that my ill-at-ease hostess did not know it yet.

"Tell me, do you have a joint?" I suddenly asked her.

Shirly was startled and said, in a high and squeaky voice, "I told you that I was finished with all that!"

"I thought that maybe you might still have some," I said – feeling doubly hopeful that she would still have at least one and that it would help keep me from drowning in the murky waters that were beginning to suffocate me.

"Do you know when I smoked my last joint?" I asked her, and answered myself right away, "when I got out of the army, I was a bit… depressed. A friend suggested that I try one and it was… um, calming. Really calming. But I gave it up not long after. I was afraid of becoming dependent on them."

She didn't react, and I could see that she preferred I go, but I didn't budge. "I'd really like to feel that way again… it's like a miracle, what it does. I'm sure you still have some, maybe two, one for me and one for you?"

She didn't say a word, but I could see her wall of resistance beginning to crack.

"I really need one," I said, continuing to badger her.

She hesitated and then finally admitted that she still had a few that she had been planning to throw away. She justified agreeing to my request by saying that she wanted to repay me for everything that I was doing for Tom. She disappeared further inside the house for a minute and returned with a rolled joint. We went out into the yard. She lit it and handed it to me. I drew on it, coughed a bit and drew on it again. After a few more hits, I handed it to her but she refused.

"Come on, take it, it's no fun to smoke alone," I urged her, but she still refused. "Tomorrow, I have a meeting with the senior social worker," she said anxiously.

"Tomorrow is tomorrow. Take it, it's no fun to smoke alone. Come on, join me."

Lately it seemed as if my conscience had become completely disassociated from my inner self, and there was nothing that would stop me from attaining my goal, regardless of how offensive it was.

Shirly hesitated but, in the end she gave in, took a hit, then another one and then gave the joint back to me. I smoked a bit more and signed for her to light another one. She refused. But once she had started, she was already into it. I took a few drags from the second joint and began laughing. Instead of bringing on the intended, calming high, I was struck by a bout of laughter.

"Did you give me a joint or laughing gas?" I said in a strangled voice.

Shirly laughed and moved in front of me like a belly dancer. We took turns taking hits, laughing and dancing. We slowly tired and I told her that there was no way I would be able to drive home now. "Can I sleep here? I saw a mattress next to Tom's bed."

Shirly didn't seem surprised nor was she put out by my request. Smoking had blurred any sense of logic for both of us.

I had barely managed to fall asleep when Tom shouted "Mommy!" in his sleep.

I sat up and caressed him. "I'm here."

Tom quieted down and went back to sleep. Then he yelled once more, again in his sleep, "Shirly, Shirly!"

Shirly swiftly ran into the room. She went to the bed and sat down next to him. "I'm here, my sweet, I'm here. Did you have a nightmare?"

"Yes… I got lost and couldn't… I called you and you didn't come…"

"It's a good thing it was only a dream, right? See, I'm right here, with you."

"Shirly, don't ever leave me," he begged.

Inside of me, everything was collapsing, but I did not dare move or make a sound.

"Of course not," she promised him. "Now close your eyes and ask for a good dream to come."

Shirly caressed his hair until his breathing became deep and regular.

"He didn't even notice that I was here," I said, softly.

"Wait till morning, he'll be surprised," she promised.

Chapter 37

I woke up at dawn. The gray light penetrated the room and formed a silver halo around Tom's face. I could have lay there forever, just looking at him, listening to his breathing, but my conscience wouldn't allow me to fully enjoy that, as it only reminded me of my three other children that I had left at home. That wasn't my fault, I declared before an imaginary judge, it's my husband's fault that I am here and not with them.

The light changed to a brighter and more yellowish hue and Tom began to stir, turning on his side, his back now turned to me. Shirly entered and saw I was already awake. She smiled at me and went to wake Tom up. The dawn's silence was broken as they both got ready for school and work. The three of us left the house together like a family on a normal morning. I got into my car, popped a refreshing mint into my mouth, and set off.

As I neared my parking space next to our building, I stopped some distance away when I saw Gil going to his car with the children; my heart tightened as I watched him put them in their car seats, one by one, belt them in and then slide behind the steering wheel. I watched as he drove away from me to drop them off at their respective kindergartens before going to his office. There he would meet Daria, the young, attractive, perfect intern who, without even knowing it, had become my bitter rival.

Half an hour later I was on my way to the plant but made a sudden U-turn and went to Ruth's office. I had to get her to do something before it was too late. I wanted Tom to sleep with me every night in the same house, that is, in my home. Shirly would just have to give birth to a child of her own.

I parked the car and went up to Ruth's office but the door was closed and her secretary said that she had someone in there with her. I sat on a chair in the small reception room next to her door and waited.

I heard Ruth's voice, then another, familiar voice: Shirly!

She beat me to it, before I had the chance to talk to Ruth, to tell her about the joints Shirly still had and how it hadn't been difficult to convince her to smoke them. To tell her how one couldn't possibly count on Shirly... but, if I went in now, Shirly would become suspicious. Ruth might even reveal who I was and then I'd lose any chance of seeing Tom, regardless of whether it was through subterfuge or honorable behavior. Why was Ruth dealing with Tom's adoption, anyway? After all, she had told me that she had agreed to resign.

The secretary entered the room to give Ruth something and, when she went out, she left the door ajar. I could hear the conversation inside.

"I only have a few more questions for you," Ruth said. "Has anyone considered the possibility that he could be placed with his other aunt, your brother-in-law's sister? After all, there, he would grow up with a family – there are siblings, two parents. It's a vibrant home."

"But with me, he'll get all my attention. After all, I've changed my whole life for him."

"What will happen if you decide to get married? Or have a child of your own?" said Ruth, asking difficult questions.

"I'm not even considering that. Why are you asking all these questions all over again?"

"I'm sorry, but I have to examine every aspect. The adoption authorities require it."

Shirly said, resentfully, "Adoption! So what if he was adopted?! He was their child! Completely theirs!"

"Of course. But I would be asking the same questions even if he were your sister's biological child," Ruth says, soothingly.

"I am certain that this is what my sister and brother-in-law would have wanted."

"What about your lifestyle? As a single parent, all the responsibility is on you, all the time."

"I swear to you that I will not touch drugs or alcohol again," said Shirly vehemently.

"How is Tom doing?" Ruth changed the subject, apparently reassured by Shirly's answers. However, soon I would be revealing the truth to her.

"He's fine. He's calmer," said Shirly earnestly. "He has even been doing his homework since Maya has been coaching him in basketball. The woman I told you about."

"She's still coming?" Ruth's voice sounded surprised but restrained.

"Sure. Yesterday, she even picked him up from school and took him home with her. Her husband played chess with him, and she…"

"Her husband?" Now Ruth sounded shocked, but Shirly didn't seem to notice and continued to tell Ruth how Tom had been excited about Gil.

Then, to Shirly's surprise on one side of the door, and my apprehension on the other, Ruth concluded the interview with a firm tone. "Fine, it looks as if we have covered everything. I will sign the papers now to confirm the adoption."

What!? I sprang up as if a wound-up coil inside of me had been released, and was just about to storm inside to break everything up, but the secretary came once again, file in hand, and entered the room. Through the almost completely open door I could hear Shirly becoming emotional, "Really? I'm so happy, Ruth. Thank you so much. I won't disappoint you! I'll be the best mother that he could ever want!"

I rose and left before I could be caught and everything would be spoiled. What should I do? How could I change Tom's fate? How could I return him to me when the whole world was against me?

I imagined all sorts of scenarios. An hour later, when I was sure that Shirly had left Ruth's office, I called Shirly and told her that the Maccabi Tel Aviv senior team was going to have a practice game that day around noon. "Tom would really enjoy watching the players; he's a big fan. I can pick him up from school and, that way, you'll have another day to get used to your new job without the pressure of having to pick him up on time," I added. I managed to convince her and she thanked me.

I pushed down my feelings of guilt from lying and scheming, both of which threatened to trigger my conscience and prevent me from carrying out my plan.

I showed up at Tom's school before the last bell had rung. His face fell when he saw that I was the one waiting for him. "Shirly couldn't come again?" he asked, frustrated.

"No, that's not it. I just wanted to take you for a day of fun!"

Still bothered by the fact that Shirly hadn't come herself, he got into my car and sat next to me. This was not the boy who had always been happy to see me when I came to his house in the afternoon to coach him.

It seemed that the many changes in his life were having an effect on him. Shirly had transformed her outward messy appearance and ostensibly abandoned her easy-going attitude overnight, turning into a serious, earnest, sober and neatly dressed woman. Maybe he really missed the cool aunt she had been until now.

For the second time in his life he was going to be adopted; but this time, he was old enough to understand, conscious that it was because of the terrible tragedy that had taken his parents from him. In spite of myself, I wondered if indeed – as Gil had told me – a judge were to ask him with whom he would like to grow up, with us or with Shirly, which would he pick?

"Where are we going?" he asked.
"For a day of fun."
"Where?"
"It's a surprise. Something that will make you very happy."
Tom shrank into himself and said that he did not like surprises.

I promised him that he would like this surprise, put my telephone on silent mode and drove to my destination, leaving the Tel Aviv area behind us as we joined the cars on route 6. I handed him a bag with some snacks and a bottle of water. The weather was kind to us – the sky was clear and blue.

"Where are we going? It seems to be very far," asked Tom for the umpteenth time as we got off the main road. I said that we would be there in a minute and finally reached our destination, a launching site for hot air balloons on Mt. Gilboa.

"Here we are!" I said in a cheerful voice. We got out of the car and then he saw it: a huge, colorful balloon, like a giant ball waiting for giant children to come and play with it.

"That's the surprise. We're going to go up together in a hot air balloon!" I told him, enthusiastically.

But my news did not have the effect that I had expected. "But *Shirly* promised me a hot air balloon! I want to do it with *her*!"

"She's very busy now at her new job. Come on. I've never been up in a hot air balloon, either."

Tom didn't move. I patted him, held his hand and, as he slowly relaxed, we approached the balloon together. The operator was waiting for us. I had reserved a private flight. We got into the basket and held onto the railing, as instructed. Very slowly, the balloon left the ground and began to rise, swinging back and forth gently.

"Are you afraid?" I was very apprehensive.

"No, not at all. It's not scary at all!" he replied sulkily, but I could hear the trembling in his voice. Below us, the checkered map of the fields in the valley became smaller and smaller.

The sun hid behind the mountain and the sky became just a bit darker.

"What a beautiful sky," I said in admiration, but really wished I could feel the ground beneath my feet.

"My father taught me about the stars," he stated, was silent for a moment and then continued, "Even now, when it's light out, the stars are in place, just like at night… you can imagine them." He closed his eyes and pointed up. "I think that the Milky Way is here… " he moved his hand, "and there is the Big Dipper… " He opened his eyes, looked at me for a split second, closed them again and continued, "Maybe the moon is over there. Yesterday, there was a full moon… " he moved his hand and said, "And here is Venus, our star," he pointed out and opened his eyes again.

"Whose?"

"Our family's star," said Tom with a dreamy expression on his face. "A year ago, we went on a trip to the Galilee, the whole family. We slept outside, under the stars. My father suggested that each one of us choose a star. I chose Venus. My mother and Shirly did, too. The three of us said 'Venus' at the same time." He told me this with an excitement tinged with sadness.

"That's a really nice name." Three girls in Dor's kindergarten had the same first name, so each had to have their last name used whenever called upon and, it would stay like that until they were the only one with that name in their class.

"Do you know what's special about it, about Venus?"

I didn't know and so, he explained it to me. "Even though it's the brightest star in the sky, we can only see it just before dawn and just after the sun sets."

I didn't say anything. The balloon was traveling eastward and the Jordan River was winding below us like a shiny, silvery snake.

"I miss my parents so much…"

I crossed my arms to prevent them from reaching out to him.

"I know that they aren't in the sky. People just say that to little children."

I wanted to say something comforting to him, something encouraging but, before I could find the proper words, he asked if he could call Shirly.

"Look at the view below," I said hurriedly, trying to distract him, but he wouldn't let up. "I want to talk to her. I want to describe all this to her."

"Tell her when we get back."

But Tom said, irritably, "You don't understand! I want to talk to her now! Without Shirly, this whole hot air balloon thing isn't worth anything."

I was silenced, astonished by his reaction. It was not what I had expected and the frustration I felt became one with the frustration I had felt during the night, when he had called out for Shirly and had only calmed down after she had talked to him, caressed him and hugged him.

I took my telephone out of the bag. As the screen came to life, it showed dozens of unanswered calls from Shirly, Gil and Ruth.

I immediately called Shirly, who answered on the first ring, and handed the phone over to Tom.

"Shirly, this isn't right. I wanted *you* to take me up in the hot air balloon!" he complained to her.

I could hear her surprise. I watched him take a selfie and send the photo to her so that she would believe that he really was floating in the sky right now.

I understood that I had lost. I realized what I had not been willing to accept the whole time – that I hadn't had a chance from the beginning. That it wasn't possible to turn back ten years of time and begin anew as if nothing had happened. I finally understood that I was fighting a losing battle, that I had been beaten and the price I would have to pay – I felt all that pain overpowering me.

Tom handed the phone back to me. In the background I could hear Gil and Ruth's voices. The three of them were there, together, because of my antics. What could Shirly be thinking, now that she knew that Ruth was my aunt? I told Shirly that I was sorry for everything, and disconnected.

Chapter 38

I already knew the way there by heart; Ruth was waiting next to the gate. She told Tom that Shirly was waiting for him inside the house and he ran across the yard. I could see Shirly coming out to meet him. They hugged as if they had not seen each other in years, and not just since that morning.

"Look at them carefully and get it through your head that she is his mother from now on," Ruth said to me firmly. "You will not see him anymore. Soon they will be moving elsewhere and, if you dare make any efforts to find them or contact him, she will file a complaint with the police. It's that simple."

"Does she know who I am? What I am to him?"

"She understands your obsession with him."

"I'm so sorry for everything."

"Me too… go home and return to your own life," she said, her voice softening, and then she suddenly embraced me. The repercussions of it all, the flash of lightning, the clap of thunder had finally ripped open the heavy, dark cloud that had been hovering over me and a torrent of tears ran down my cheeks. I hugged her back.

It was already late when I got home, hung my bag on the hook and came into the dark living room where the television screen was flickering.

Gil was sitting on the couch and, without looking at me, asked me what I was doing there.

I tried to tell him that I was sorry, but he wasn't moved by my words.

"Are you finished kidnapping children?" he berated me.
"I'm so sorry. For everything. Really."
"It's too late."
"Gil…"
"Take this, it arrived by messenger for you."
I glanced at the envelope in his hand and said that it didn't matter anymore.
Gil pushed the envelope into my hand. "Doesn't matter? You don't want to know anything about his DNA?"
I tore the envelope up into little pieces. "No. You were right. He has a family and it's not this one."
He was silent.
"I want to come home. To come back to you."
"I can't look at you."
I was confused, certain that it had been a slip of the tongue and, any minute now, he would take back what he said, but he continued to stare at the screen in silence.
"Because I wanted Tom?"
"Because you do whatever you want, without a single thought about what I might want!"
"That's not true!" I shouted.
"It's true and it's always been that way. I blocked it out, I ignored it, but now I want to get as far away as possible from you!"
"Gil, don't say that…"
He cut me off with an irritated gesture and words gushed out like an erupting geyser. "When you decided to give birth at the age of 18, you ignored my feelings, my thoughts, what I wanted, as if they weren't important. When you wanted us to get married and have children right away, you ignored the fact that I wanted to wait until after I had completed my studies and taken the bar exam. Afterwards, for years, you tried to find the boy, because that's what *you* wanted, and you hid that from me."
"Gil…"

"Look where your obsession to bring that child back to you has brought us."

"But it's all over. I won't pursue it anymore. I realize that I was wrong."

"It's too late. You lied to me, over and over again."

"Only about this. I never lied to you about anything else!" I protested in desperation.

"I can't trust you," he said, in a cold and distant voice.

"You can! Please, Gil, I'm so sorry for what happened. I'm sorry, I'm sorry..."

He had to forgive me so that we could reconcile, like after any other argument, but he was silent.

"So, what will happen now?" I asked, afraid of the answer. Afraid that he would say that he was leaving me.

"I don't know. Maybe nothing. Time will tell."

I felt a dark abyss open up under my feet, a terrifying emptiness that I thought would swallow me whole. I couldn't even cry. There were no tears left in me.

Chapter 39

Gil allowed me to come home "for the sake of the children." One day followed the other and an automatic and uninspired routine fell into place. Once again, I tried to take an active part in the daily activities of the house and made an effort to see my family as a whole rather than as if a part of it was missing. But at night, I would fall into a restless sleep.

Gil returned to the bedroom after Dor and Shai asked why Daddy was sleeping in the living room, but he used a separate blanket, not allowing for any chance contact which might show me that his body had forgiven me and that the heart and mind would follow. Instead, the two of us lay on separate sides of the bed, each huddled under his and her own blanket, like two snails that happened to wander into the same field, falling asleep and waking up without invading the other's personal space.

I kept telling myself that time would work its magic, holding onto that hope to prevent me from collapsing into despair. I was sure that, in time, the bitter taste of what I had done would fade away and he would miss me. It couldn't happen any other way. But days passed and Gil remained aloof.

He came home from the office in time to be with the children. We were very polite to one another but as our façade of civility became more sophisticated, the distance between us increased. We only spoke when necessary with regards to matters of the home or the children, communicating as little as possible and showing zero emotional connection.

I barely slept at night. I would listen to Gil's deep breathing and was filled with resentment that he was able to sleep. I would pace among the rooms, listening to the boys' gentle breathing and to the sound of Ya'ara's breaths making their way through the maze of her nasal cavities, and return to the bedroom. Gil slept on his back. The room itself was in pitch darkness and his face was barely visible in the weak light that came in from the hall. I stood over him for several minutes, hoping, in vain, that he would open his eyes.

In the plant, the routine, for the most part, remained unchanged. Several candidates for the position of Operations Manager had been interviewed, but Eric couldn't make up his mind about a worthy replacement for his brother. Eric and I were interacting with each other with propriety. A silent agreement had been made not to talk about what had happened on our fun day and, with time, our personal relationship had vanished. Perhaps he had thought that something might happen in the spa hotel and was disappointed; or, since he was the only son left to carry the load, the weighty responsibility of running the plant caused him to focus solely on work.

"What's the matter with you? You look as if you're in mourning," Elena said to me one day. I didn't respond. I couldn't contradict her, but neither did I want to confirm what she said. How can one mourn a child who is alive? Or a marriage that is hanging on by a thread?

She shrugged her shoulders and asked, "Tell me, haven't you noticed anything different about me?"

I hastily looked in her direction and she pirouetted in front of me on two long legs wrapped in a pair of tight jeans.

"How could I not have noticed? What happened?" I asked her.

"I have a boyfriend and he doesn't like when I wear a mini-skirt to work," she answered, her voice secretly expressing delight.

"So what now? Do you think that they won't come to the window of the control room now?" I said, half-jokingly.

"They have to come. Because of the standards," she announced cheerfully.

She seemed to have forgotten all her complaining when she had to work alone at the control window while I was writing the book on procedures.

I smiled at her in spite of myself.

"Admit it, I'm a good influence on you," she said, winking at me.

Chapter 40

The vast emptiness that had become a recurrent part of my day became crowded with thoughts. I undertook an examination of my past, poking through it like an archeologist, trying to comprehend each decision, deed or action that I had taken. I spread the last ten years before me like a rug, tearing it apart, thread by thread, examining the choice of pattern, matching the colors. I put pieces of our lives under a magnifying glass and examined them with the dispassionate eye of a scientist.

I wasn't in any rush to come to conclusions or to share my thoughts with Gil. We were like two trains which, by pure luck, managed not to collide. I certainly did not want to risk that. I didn't know whether or not Ruth had told my parents what had happened, if she had, once again, spoken to them behind my back but, based on their behavior, I guessed that she had not told them about my shenanigans over the past few months.

My parents sensed that something was off. Worried, my mother asked me what was happening with us and I calmed her down, telling her that everything was fine, just some pressure at work. The lie rolled off my tongue without any effort and I asked myself what would happen if the ability to lie without blinking an eye became second nature to me. Maybe it already had, and that scared me.

My father mentioned to Gil that it had been a long time since we'd gone on a family outing together, and he suggested that we should go on one soon, before the summer heat made it nearly impossible. Dor and Shai heard their grandfather and backed him up, crying out, "Outing! Outing!" and then Ya'ara chimed in, jumping up and down in excitement.

Gil promised to plan something for the coming weekend; and so, on Saturday morning, we took the car to the Menashe hills and parked the car in the lot at the start of the hike. The magnificent sight of fields of poppies and chrysanthemums, spread out as far as the eye could see, simply took our breaths away. The reds and yellows merging together and the children running around in the open was beautiful. My father said that it was lucky that the flowers had bloomed late this year, otherwise the poppies wouldn't have been around anymore.

My mother sat down in the middle of a patch of chrysanthemums, picked a few dozen blooms and made a yellow chain. "Do you remember that I taught you how to make these once?" she asked me enthusiastically. As I followed her rapidly moving fingers, I recalled that she had, in fact, taught me, but I had never really been good at it. She finished two yellow chains, stood up, put one around my neck, and extended the other one to Gil. "I can't reach your neck." He was embarrassed and tried to put it around her neck, but she moved her head aside and insisted that he put it on. "These chains bring luck and blessings," she said, accentuating her words.

"Mother!" I said, surprised. Since when did she believe in things like that?

She felt that something wasn't right between us. I couldn't look her in the eye. Maybe there was something to what she had said? I gleaned hope from what my mother, the retired scientist, had said and suddenly, impulsively, took the flower chain from Gil's hands, raised myself on my toes, and put it over his head. Now we were both wearing flower chains that were supposed to bring luck and blessings. For just a moment, I believed that they would bring about a miracle, that Gil would shed the resentment that he had towards me and would love me again as before, but he turned away and asked if anyone was hungry, suggesting that we get the cooler, spread the picnic blanket under the eucalyptus tree at the edge of the flowering field, and eat the lunch we had packed.

On the way home, I stroked the flower chains, mine and his, that were laying on my chest and said to myself that I had to find a way back into Gil's heart. I repeated that over and over again, silently, like a mantra. But how? I had already tried everything...

Late that night, after too many vain attempts to fall asleep, I sat down at the kitchen table; it occurred to me that maybe I could write him a letter. Yes, that's what I would do. I would write him a letter – on paper. Not through WhatsApp or email, but a real letter, like in the olden days. I would pour my heart out in a one-sided conversation. That way he wouldn't be able to answer me straightaway and reject everything I had to say outright: the apology, the explanations, the admission of having done wrong, asking for his forgiveness.

I took pen to paper and tried to express my feelings. I crossed out sentences and paragraphs, crumbled up page after page and threw them out and, in the end, realized that I would not be able to write anything that would truly express what I wanted to say, something that would touch him.

My eyes turned towards a glass bowl that I had filled with water and placed on the counter. The lucky yellow flower chains that my mother had made were there, side by side, floating in the water, winking at me in silent consolation.

Seder night came. That year it was our turn to celebrate at my parents' home. They also invited Gil's parents, since his brother and family had flown to Thailand 'to get away from this holiday' and they would be alone. If only I too could have escaped this crowded family evening. Nonetheless, Gil and I cooperated and put on a show for our four parents, doing our best to keep the cracks that were threatening to break us up, break up our family, hidden.

As usual, Ruth also came, bringing her salads and the cake she had made straight to the kitchen. In the past, when my grandparents were still alive, these family events had been difficult for her as she felt she had failed to live up to their expectations, again and again, of finally finding someone with whom she could raise a family. After one particularly frustrating holiday dinner, when my grandmother couldn't help herself and clearly expressed her disappointment in Ruth and 'suggesting' that she stop being so choosy, she stopped coming to family meals and would make other plans on New Year's and Passover, primarily to distance herself as much as possible from the family that was suffocating her.

After she and my mother had been orphaned, Ruth started celebrating with us again and, ever since Dor's birth, had become a kind of second grandmother to our children. At times, when she was able to get away from her demanding job, she would even come visit us, as she put it, just to 'sniff' them.

I followed her into the kitchen and hugged her. She hugged me back and didn't let go. My mother wondered what this meant, what looked more like a 'goodbye' hug, and asked her sister if she was going anywhere. Ruth straightened up and said, "No. I'm not going anywhere, but I am taking early retirement." She then added, "which means that from now on, you will have to share your quality time with the children with me because I plan on spending a lot more time with them."

For just a moment, my mother was quiet and looked at her sister suspiciously, questioning the reason behind this surprise retirement, but Ruth went on to tell us both about the new life she had all planned out.

"I'm really looking forward to an end of the obligations and responsibilities. You and I," she said, turning to my mother, "will be able to spend more time together now that we're both retired. Two free women who will change the world!" she ended, excitedly.

My mother didn't have a chance to recover from her surprise and join in on Ruth's enthusiasm when my father called us to the table to start reading the Passover Haggadah before the little ones became too impatient.

My mother's lucky yellow chains began to wilt. Gil threw them out and poured out the water that had started to smell bad. I told myself that they were only chrysanthemums that, unfortunately, they couldn't bring about the miracle I had been waiting for, but such is life.

I couldn't get over the fear that Gil might tire of this static situation and decide to leave home. I was worried about the fact that he was in contact with Daria every day, at the office and did not dare ask about her. When I dreaded that he would abandon me, I would think, in desperation, about all types of women with whom he had been in contact, even that client with the long hair who had been sitting with him in David's restaurant, together with her son. I berated myself for this and tried to be encouraged by the fact that he was trying to maintain a set routine that did not arouse any suspicion.

During especially difficult days, I focused upon the many good times we had shared during our first "chapter," and in particular, during the second one. I convinced myself that these were also stored in his memories and that in the end, they would defeat the bad memories, and that our love would sweep away the oppressive residues, purify his spirit that would then, once more, open itself to my love.

Time continued at its own tempo, without taking our feelings into account. I kept on telling myself that something good would eventually happen. Something that would break the ice and close the cracks that had formed between us.

In the meantime, I told myself that I would stick to our civil routine which kept us together, at least in the same house, and would be satisfied with joint parenting, doing things that had to be done around the house and for the children that we shared. Until something good happened…

Summer came and took over our lives. Nights became longer, warmer and the duvets were placed on the top shelves in the closet. Gil took down a lighter blanket for himself, a single blanket, and I used a flat sheet that I had once taken from my parents' house. Our summer blanket for two remained in the cupboard.

It was an especially hot summer night and, once again – like on most nights – I found it difficult to fall asleep. Our room was not completely dark, the way it had been before the children were born. We kept the door open and the small night light in the hallway next to the children's room shone in. I lay on my back and stared at the blades of the ceiling fan over our bed, turning round and round in a misguided attempt to circulate the hot air, until I became hypnotized by it and finally fell into a much-needed sleep.

The fan's efforts failed miserably and during the night, Gil and I both threw off our covers – he the light blanket and me the sheet. Then his body and mine, spontaneously and with mixed feelings, touched. It was like two old friends who hadn't met for some time getting to know one another once more, communicating in their own, private language, bonded by a familiar desire that had lay dormant for some time. Our spirits were sleepy, but our physical beings were awakened.

My eyes were first to open. It was early. A pale light came in through the window via the partially closed blinds. My head was lying on Gil's arm. We were both naked under the single blanket. I was embarrassed, as if I had been caught with a strange man in my bed, wanting to caress his chest but restraining myself. I didn't dare move.

Ya'ara's voice came from the children's room. She always was the first out of the three to rise. For her, Saturday morning was no different than any weekday morning. Gil woke up, freed his arm from beneath my head and rushed to pull his shorts on. "Get dressed, she'll be coming in soon," he said, in a businesslike tone. Poof! The magic was gone, as if what had happened under the cover of darkness and half-sleep hadn't happened. When Ya'ara stumbled into the room, armed with her pacifier and her cloth blankie, we were once again the efficient parents.

We had promised the children that we would spend Saturday at the sea and drove to our favorite spot that had many small bays, where the water was shallow and calm, so that the children could play around and splash relatively safely. Many families like ours would come there, mothers and fathers watching their children from afar or playing with them in the shallow water. As far as I was concerned, all the others were transparent and only our children existed. And Gil. I tried to catch his eye to no avail. I refused to give up. I was certain that, under the anger and iciness, he still loved me. It couldn't be any other way. I told myself that what had happened during the night would surely happen again until, little by little, his spirit would mesh with his body and it, too, would forgive me.

Until something good happens.

Thank you to my family, nuclear and extended, for your support and encouragement during the various writing stages; and to my friends, for reading the manuscript and providing constructive criticism that undoubtedly contributed to the final result.

Printed in Great Britain
by Amazon